TRICK OF THE EYE

Pam Clifford

Trick of the Eye
Copyright © 2021 Pam Clifford

The right of Pam Clifford to be identified as the Author of the Work has been asserted by her in accordance with the Copyright, Designs and Patents Act 1988.

All the characters in this book are fictitious and any resemblance to actual persons, living or dead, is purely coincidental.

Any unauthorised broadcasting, public performance, copying or recording will constitute an infringement of copyright. No part of this book may be reproduced or transmitted in any form or by any means, electronically or mechanical, including photocopying, fax, data transmittal, internet site, recording or any information storage or retrieval system without the express permission of the author.

All rights reserved

To my family

I recognised her straight away. She's hardly changed since I last saw her all those years ago. Her hair is shorter, but those eyes, those beautiful brown eyes, still sparkle and her smile lights up the room. She may have moved on but I have never forgotten her.

She didn't recognise me. How could she when she barely knew I existed back then.

But fate has brought her back to me and this time I will not let her go

CHAPTER 1

Saturday August 31st

Chloe set off in her little Fiat to the Saturday morning Park Run which was held in the nearby small town of Forest-in-the-Green. A rental van was parked next to her car on the drive of the red brick converted school where she lived, and she wondered if the new neighbour was moving in today. The ground floor flat had been on the market for a while, but the sign had recently changed to declare that it had been sold. She was surprised that it had taken so long as it was a lovely spacious apartment. Much as she would have liked it, Chloe hadn't been able to afford the bigger flat on her salary.

It was a beautiful late August morning and a majestic red kite rode the thermals looking for its breakfast over the newly-harvested fields. As she approached the edge of town, Chloe slowed to pull into the park.

She set her watch to record her time, and headed off along the five kilometre course through the pleasant landscape. She had taken up running gradually about a year ago by using the 'Couch to 5K' app before joining the weekly Park Run. She felt much fitter now and it had been good for her figure too. It helped to run with other like-minded people who were at a similar level. Jeremy, who had only been coming to the park for a couple of weeks, and was still rather overweight, was trying to keep up with her today, but she soon put some distance between them. She beat her personal best and would be able to impress her friends on Facebook later.

Returning home, Chloe parked up next to the transit van and cast a glance through the window of the ground floor flat as she made her way to her front door, which was tucked away to the left of the main sturdy oak portal; but there was no-one about.

She nudged the door closed and threw her grubby trainers into the small under-stairs cupboard before making her way to the bathroom for a warm shower.

Refreshed and dressed in black jeans and her favourite jade top - which went so well with her auburn hair - she looked down at her black leather shoes and decided she would have to replace them in the near future. Today she was going into Birmingham to get some new clothes for work, so she could take in a few shoe shops along the way. The weather was soon going to turn cooler and she needed to be prepared.

She wasn't fond of driving in heavy traffic, but there

was a bus into the city at eleven thirty; she should have no trouble catching that.

As she passed the living room window, which looked out to the front of the house, she could see the jeans-clad rear end of someone who was leaning into the back of the van to drag something out. She paused long enough to see a rather good-looking guy with short, wavy fair hair emerge, holding a Z-bed which he carried towards the house. *If he's sleeping on that he must be waiting for his furniture to arrive*, she thought, *or he's buying new.*

Just as she stepped out of the house, she heard the old school door click shut. She had missed her chance to get a proper look at him. It would have been good to have had the opportunity to introduce herself and welcome him to his new home.

Chloe arrived home with five carrier bags - always a sign of a good shopping trip. She saw something move out of the corner of her eye and realised the man from the ground floor flat was standing looking out of his living room window. He was taller than she had originally thought and quite good looking too. With her hands full she could only manage a smile before dumping her carriers onto the doorstep and struggling to get her keys from her handbag. He nodded in response and turned away.

She changed into a comfortable pair of joggers and busied herself in hanging up her new clothes while she waited for her meal - a moussaka she had bought in

Marks and some chips from the freezer - to heat up in the oven.

As she was just scraping up the last bit of sauce with a chip, her mobile rang. She picked it up from the worktop where she had left it on charge earlier in the day.

"Hi Alex, everything okay?"

"Chloe! Where have you been? I've been ringing all afternoon. I've been dying to tell you my news. Giles and I have set a wedding date!"

"That's fantastic! Congratulations! So - when and where?"

"We've been to look at Chippington Hall this morning, and we've set the date for Friday, May 29th."

"Oh, that's a lovely place. I remember the cricket club used to hold their annual fete in the parkland there. The landscaped grounds will make a good backdrop for the photos."

"Yes. I've always liked it, with its pretty little church. It just seemed the ideal place. Now I need to ask you a favour."

"What's that?"

"I'd like you to be my chief bridesmaid."

"Of course I will! I would be honoured!"

"I promise I won't have you dressed up like a little princess! In fact it would be great if you come over one day soon and help me choose my dress, and the bridesmaids' dresses."

"I'm free most Saturdays. I can miss Park Run for one week."

"That's great! Would the weekend after next be okay?"

Chloe grabbed her handbag and took out her little diary. "Yes, that will be fine - I can catch an early train."

"I'll be in touch nearer the time to arrange everything."

"Okay - speak to you soon. Give my love to Giles!"

Chloe placed her phone on the table and poured herself a glass of wine – after all, this was a celebration. Alex and Giles had been living together for ages and she knew that they would one day tie the knot, but it was a lovely surprise all the same.

She picked up the television remote control and flicked through the stations but couldn't find anything that took her fancy so decided on some music. She soon found her playlist which she had entitled 'Latin American', which suited her mood. Dancing around the living room, tidying as she went, she sang along at full volume as she plumped the cushions and sorted through the magazine pile in readiness for Mick's imminent arrival. She belatedly remembered that there was someone living downstairs now and realised she would need to tone it down a bit, and she changed the music to something gentler and quieter.

It was about eight o'clock when she heard her doorbell.

"It looks like someone has moved in downstairs," Mick said. "I had to park the van out in the road."

"Yes. I saw a young guy, about our age, when I looked out earlier," she said as she led the way back up to her flat.

Mick had been to watch his football team win and was in a jubilant mood. Chloe told him about her sister's wedding plans as she fetched him a beer from the fridge. She poured a bag of kettle chips into a large bowl and set it on the coffee table for them to share as they settled down to stream the next episode of a thriller they had been watching on catch-up. It ended on another cliff-hanger and they would have to wait until next week to watch the next episode.

"Did you do Park Run this morning?" he asked

"Yes. With all the excitement of the wedding I forgot to tell you. I got a personal best -although I think it might have been because that Jeremy guy was standing right behind me at the start. He was too close, you know, invading my space. I was glad to show him a clean pair of heels."

"I think he fancies you," Mick teased, his brown eyes twinkling below his mop of dark wavy hair.

"Lord, I hope not - he gives me the creeps."

"He's harmless enough really," he said, taking a swig from his bottle. "Just a bit molly-coddled by his mother, I think. He's got an amazing knack for doing the scoring at darts - he can subtract as fast as anyone I know."

"He must be okay then," she said with a wry look.

CHAPTER 2

Sunday September 1st

Mick was first to wake up to the sound of someone drilling. He reached down to pick up his phone from the floor by the bed. It was only eight o'clock.

"Someone likes to get up early," he muttered when the noise started again.

"Mm." Chloe stretched sleepily.

"He's not the only one," he grinned as he grabbed her playfully.

Chloe pretended to be annoyed but her sparkling eyes gave her away.

"I'm absolutely starving," he declared a little while later.

"I've got eggs and bacon if you'd like?"

"That would be awesome. I think I'll nip to the shop and get a paper while you're cooking."

"Could you bring some milk? We're a bit short."

Chloe put the frying pan to work, heated some water ready to poach the eggs, and slotted seeded brown bread into the toaster. She was setting the small kitchen table when Mick returned.

"I have just been speaking to your new neighbour, Bob."

"What was he doing, drilling at this time on a Sunday morning?"

"Fitting a security light. Apparently he's only going to be here at weekends as he rents near his work in the week, so he wants to keep the place safe while he's away - make it look lived in. Wait for this though: he's only going to be commuting to Amsterdam!"

"That's rather a long way to go to work."

"I said that, but he says it's not a problem, as he's able to take an early flight out from Birmingham on a Monday morning and there's one back on a Friday evening."

"I wonder why he decided to come here to buy."

"Said he wants to move back to England eventually, to somewhere central. Being so near to the airport is ideal. It's perfect for him, and great for you too - you can make as much noise as you like during the week." He grinned as he took his seat at the table.

"So what's he like?" Chloe asked as she squirted brown sauce onto her eggs.

"Okay, I guess. He's very well spoken - made me feel like a right country bumpkin. But do you know what's strangest of all?"

She shook her head.

"He doesn't like football, or any other sport for that matter. I've never met a man who didn't like sport before."

Chloe laughed.

By the time they left the house later in the morning, Bob had finished his DIY, for now at least, so Chloe still didn't get a chance to meet him.

They were heading to Bulls Cross where the annual fete was being held. Chloe offered to drive; having a small car had its advantages, and she was more likely to be able to find a parking space on the grass verge than Mick would in his van.

As they walked towards the village green the smell of the hog roast was so inviting that Mick was very soon in the queue, while Chloe found them somewhere to sit on a straw bale which had been set up for spectators of the dog show later. A happy Mick ambled over with a large pork bap in each hand. As he approached, he noticed Jeremy heading their way and abruptly changing direction.

"I think your mate was coming to see you just now," Mick nodded towards the portly figure moving in the direction of the cake stall.

"It's a good job you came back when you did then. Thank you," she added as she took the serviette-covered offering.

They enjoyed a spot of people watching as they

munched their rolls, then wandered off to join the queue at the tombola stall, where Mick won a bottle of English white wine. They enjoyed the dog show with all its different categories, and Chloe fell in love with the little dachshund which was declared the winner of the waggiest tail competition. She was delighted to win a big teddy bear in the raffle, and Mick kindly offered to carry it for the rest of the afternoon. They mingled and chatted with villagers and enjoyed a glass of cold cider in the garden of the Bull.

Back at the car once more, Chloe placed the teddy bear onto the back seat, and as they headed for home, they agreed that it had been a good afternoon.

The hired Transit was not there when they pulled into the drive, so Mick went outside and reversed his van in off the road. Chloe was waiting when he jumped out of the driving seat.

"Someone's knocked your indicator and broken the lens." She pointed at the rear driver's side.

"There was plenty of room to get past," Mick grumbled as he looked to make sure there was no more damage. "It must have happened here. I'm sure it was all right when I left home last night.

CHAPTER 3

Saturday September 14th

Mick drove Chloe to New Street station to catch her train. He could leave his plumber's van at the home of his mate's parents in Small Heath while he and Pete took the supporters' coach to the match in London, and Chloe and Alex were hoping for an enjoyable day looking at wedding dresses.

Chloe was pleased to see he had given the cab a good clear out after work yesterday, as often she had to move bits of pipe or paperwork onto the floor before she could sit down. She'd dressed smartly and didn't want grease on her clean trousers.

The train to Cheltenham was due in fifteen minutes and, according to the big departures board, was on time, but she could still call in at Cafe Nero before descending to the platform. As she was waiting at the counter she glanced around and saw someone she thought she knew, but couldn't for the life of her think who. The man seemed to be watching her intently, but didn't acknowledge her. Perhaps he was similarly uncertain whether he knew her. Just then, the cashier asked for her order, and by the time she looked again he was gone. She took her drink and made her way across the bright airy concourse, through the baffle-gate turnstile and on to the escalator which led down to the dark, dingy platform.

The train was on time as promised and she quickly found a table seat that wasn't already booked and plonked herself down next to the window. Opposite her was a plump, middle-aged lady deeply engrossed in a book. Chloe noticed it was a novel by her favourite author and was tempted to say how much she had enjoyed it, but she didn't want to interrupt such intense reading. She finished her coffee as they glided out of the city and turned her attention to the world outside the carriage. They sped past the bright purple-painted station at Bourneville, and the urban sprawl was soon replaced by fields of cattle and sheep, and a distant village clustered round a church tower. Now and then cuttings obscured her view, then a river would meander by, and before long there was the unmistakable sight of Cleeve Hill, standing guard over Cheltenham Racecourse.

Her sister waved to her as she stepped onto Platform One. It was great to see her; it had been a while since her last trip home. They hugged then hurried out to find their mother's black Kia turning into the car park. She hadn't been able to find a space and had been forced to drive round the block. The conversation on the short journey into town centred on the lack of parking, the price of the invitations, and how their dad had a new hobby, which she would learn about later. Chloe was already aware of how many bridal shops there were to visit and was really looking forward to helping her sister choose her dress and maybe finding something decent to wear herself.

After a morning surrounded by organza, taffeta and lace, Alex had found her dream dress. It was a simple A-line ankle-length satin dress with embroidered bodice and sweetheart neckline, and Chloe was almost in tears when she saw her sister wearing it. She hadn't found anything suitable among the bridesmaid's dresses but said she would have a look online to see if there was anything she liked there. Her sister reminded her that it had to be a colour that would also be suitable for Giles' nine-year-old dark-haired niece, Becky.

Cheerful but tired, the three ladies made their way up the Promenade to the Montpellier district and found a new bistro where they were lucky enough to get a table. It was good to be able to relax and to talk about something other than dresses.

"That was a good morning's work," Alex exclaimed as she studied the menu.

The other two readily agreed.

"It's so good to be spending the day together with

both of my daughters," their mother said as the waitress came for their drinks order. "I think we should have a glass of Prosecco while we wait for our starters."

The glasses of sparkling wine arrived quickly and the food was duly ordered.

"So what's all this about Dad and his new hobby?" Chloe asked.

"He won a photo workshop with Ted Sharpe, down at the nature reserve," her mother explained. "Now he's really fired up and has started an Instagram account where he uploads his snaps. The ones he took with the professional were really quite good and I don't have the heart to tell him the ones he's taken since haven't been anywhere near up to the mark."

"And he's talking about saving money on a photographer by taking the wedding photos himself," added Alex, rolling her eyes. "We need to talk him out of that one."

Chloe told them about her work at Beeches Animal Farm.

"James has given me free rein to update the website and I've been busy putting together some new information packs which I can send out to groups who have been before, and to new enquirers."

"It must be so satisfying to have a job you really enjoy," Alex said.

"Yes, it is, and no two days are the same. I cover quite a few different people when they are on holiday or sick. One day I'm in the office, another I could be feeding the pigs, and then I usually do the educational talks. It suits me down to the ground. How's your job going now, Sis?"

"It's okay," Alex replied with a shrug. "I've always enjoyed working at Looking Good because I love chatting to the customers and helping them to find the perfect item, but now the owner wants us to sell add-ons which I don't like at all. It's horrible having to try to flog things to people that they don't really want or need."

They were still talking half an hour after they had finished eating and Chloe realised that she needed to get to the station to catch her train.

"I wish I could stay over with you tonight, Mum," Chloe said as she hugged her, " but Mick's borrowing his dad's car and picking me up early tomorrow. We're taking his nephew to Longleat while the weather is still good."

"Perhaps next time," her mother replied. "We had better head back to the car."

It wasn't a very pleasant journey home. The train was late and there were no seats available in the first two carriages. She finally found one next to a teenage mum who was bouncing a red-faced baby on her knee. As she sat down the child spat its dummy out and it landed in Chloe's lap before rolling onto the floor. She retrieved it from under the seat in front and handed it back to the child's mother, who didn't seem in the least grateful. Chloe was tired, her feet hurt, the carriage was hot and stuffy and the unrelenting screaming from the little darling next to her resulted in her having the most dreadful headache by the time she fought her way onto the crowded platform.

She headed straight to Boots for some paracetamol before nipping into Marks' Simply Food outlet to buy a ready-made sandwich and a bottle of wine for later. She couldn't face doing a grocery shop tonight.

It was already quite dusky when Chloe left the bus, which had taken the long villages route to the hamlet she called home. She was nearly blinded when the bright security light flashed on as she approached her door and shielded her eyes. She supposed it would be good later in the year when she came home from work in the dark.

Bob must have seen the light go on because she could see his outline behind the window in the unlit room, obviously checking who was there. Chloe waved to show she had seen him and he waved back, but he made no move to come out and meet her.

She kicked off her shoes as soon as she reached the landing and placed them on the shoe rack. It had been an enjoyable but tiring day and she decided a long soak in the bath would be good. She might even light some scented candles.

CHAPTER 4

Sunday September 15th

Paula White had secured a place at Bristol university to study for a BA in Archaeology and Anthropology. A childhood interest in objects such as pieces of old china plates, keys and bones which she had dug up while playing in the garden had been fuelled by learning about the Romans at school.

Today her parents had brought her along with all her important possessions to the student house where she planned to live for the next three years . She was a very shy nine-teen-year-old and didn't make friends easily so it wasn't surprising that she had made sure to pack her diary.

I am here at last, sitting on my newly made bed with my

brand new bright purple bedding, wondering what on earth I am doing here. Have I done the right thing coming to university in this strange city or would I have been better off getting a job near the comfort of my own home, like Jan? Mum and Dad have just left and I miss them already. I'm excited but scared at the same time.

There are five other rooms in this house. Two were already taken by students who will be in their second year. One of them was Beth who I met once when we came to look at the house all those months ago.

The house is very quiet and I don't think anyone else has arrived yet. I wonder what they will all be like.

I'll pop home next weekend. I may go to Jan's birthday disco – well, she did invite me. I wonder if Martin will be there.

CHAPTER 5

Saturday September 21st

Saturday night already. Chloe had been surfing the net all afternoon. She had started by looking for dresses, and had progressed through jewellery and then onto boots and had completely lost track of the time. Now she was rushing around getting ready to go out and was making the finishing touches to her make-up when the doorbell rang.

She grabbed her jacket and handbag and raced downstairs where Mick was waiting on the doorstep. She hadn't seen him since Wednesday night. He usually came over on a Friday, but last night he had been out with an old school friend who was home from France visiting his parents.

"I've missed you," she said as he hugged her.

"You're wearing perfume," he murmured.

"Yes - I'm impressed that you noticed. It came in the post the other day. I think it must have been a free sample – I click on so many offers and competitions. Nice surprise though."

Tonight they were going to see the new Will Smith thriller in Hartleigh. As they were meeting friends afterwards for a drink, they were travelling by bus and would find a cab when they were ready to return home.

They walked hand in hand to the bus stop and didn't have to wait long before the number 12 came into view. Mick paid the driver while Chloe found a quiet seat near the back. When he sat down, Mick put his arm along the back of the seat squeezing her shoulder gently and she snuggled up closer to him.

"The film should be good from what I've seen of the trailer," he said.

Chloe agreed. She liked Will Smith so would enjoy it whatever.

As they drew near the park, on the edge of Forest-in-the-Green, Chloe told him that Jeremy had walked straight up to her that morning before the run and dared to ask her where she had been the week before.

"As if it is any of his business. He told me I shouldn't miss a week or before long, when the weather was colder or wet I would use any excuse to not go. Cheeky bugger!"

"Aww, he obviously missed you," Mick teased her, but on seeing her stern face kissed her forehead.

She smiled.

"I guess it's my own fault. I spoke to him the first

time he turned up because I recognised him from the pub - tried to make him feel welcome. Now he always makes a bee-line for me."

"It was your friendly, outgoing nature that I first noticed about you, so I can't blame him if he has a crush on you," he laughed.

"I just find him a bit creepy."

"Talking of creepy," he said, suddenly serious, "I think I was being followed on Wednesday night when I left yours."

"You were rather late leaving. Perhaps it was the police keeping an eye on you. Or more likely, you were imagining it."

"Dunno. The lanes were quiet but a car seemed to take every turn the same as me. It wasn't close and I wouldn't have noticed if it hadn't had those halogen lights, which were shining straight into my wing mirror and half blinding me."

"Why would anyone want to follow you?"

He shrugged, and decided to let it go. "You're right - it must have been that weird cop film we were watching that got to me." He pressed the buzzer and the bus soon came to a halt at their stop.

After the film they headed to the Dog and Bone where they quickly located Pete and Karen by the staircase in the corner.

"Hi. How're you doing?" Chloe greeted them.

Seeing that their glasses were nearly empty Mick asked them what they were drinking before heading to the bar. Chloe put her jacket over the chair next to Karen's and sat down.

"Phew, it's warm in here." She picked up a beer mat and started to fan her face with it.

"There's quite a crowd tonight. It was hard to find a seat," Karen said.

"How was the film?" Pete asked.

"It was really good." Chloe proceeded to tell them more about it, being careful not to spoil the plot.

Pete, who wasn't a fan of the cinema and preferred to wait until the film came out on DVD, thought it sounded like one for his collection in a few months' time.

Mick returned carrying a tray loaded with drinks and some bags of crisps which he placed on the table before sitting next to Pete.

The friends chatted amicably and it wasn't long before Mick and Pete were debating a rather controversial penalty in the United game.

Raising her eyebrows and shaking her head Karen turned to Chloe.

"It's my birthday next Saturday, and as the boys will be at an away game, I thought it would be nice if we could meet up for afternoon tea."

"I'd really like that. Had you anywhere in mind?"

"Yes. There's a new, rather unique cafe aptly named The PM Tea Shop. They've been getting great reviews for their mouth-watering cakes."

"It sounds wonderful. I never could resist a good cake."

"I was thinking of tea at three, then we'll have plenty of time before we meet the boys later."

"That sounds perfect to me."

"I'll get on and book it."

The Dog and Bone could be relied on for entertainment on a Saturday night and tonight was no exception. A young blonde girl - Maddie Mae - was singing songs ranging from the sixties to more up-to-date which covered the tastes of most of the clientele.

It seemed no time at all before last orders were called and the four friends were leaving along with the rest, some of them still singing the chorus of the last song of the evening, 'I Knew You Were Trouble,' although their rendition of the Taylor Swift song wasn't as in tune as Maddie had sung it.

The late night fish and chip shop was on the way to the taxi rank in the main street and they wandered in for bags of chips before parting company and going their own separate ways.

Mick and Chloe sat on a bench to eat their supper. The evening had been quite warm for the time of year but there was now a chilly breeze and Chloe pulled her coat round her tightly. It had been a good night, but she would be glad to get home now.

CHAPTER 6

Friday September 27th

I am home for the weekend. It is Jan's birthday and I'm going to her party tomorrow night at the social club. I've missed my bestie and although we text all the time, it will be wonderful to see her. She has invited Martin and he's told her he will be there. Maybe, just maybe he will notice me.

The train journey home today was interesting. I caught the First Western from Temple Meads. A rather scruffy individual with a beard sat opposite picking at the skin near his fingernails. There was nowhere to move to so I was glad when he stood up to leave as we pulled into Cheltenham Spa station. A man in an old tweed jacket and dark rimmed spectacles took the seat. He held a carrier from Next and was quite good looking but he had steely grey eyes. He didn't stay long, as when the train began to speed up he got up and left the carriage. A little while later a real hunk took up the seat. He was smartly dressed, in a trendy, dark blue suit. He didn't have a tie but had the top button of his shirt open. His hair had blond highlights. Well, I've always had a thing about eyes and he had the most beautiful deep blue eyes. He noticed me gaping at him and smiled; I must have gone as red as a beetroot. He had a little black overnight case which he hugged on his lap. At New Street station everyone had to get off and I found myself jostled along by the crowd. I've decided that I don't like New Street - it's too big. I was scared I would miss my connection, but I didn't. Mum was waiting for me at Tamworth. Today I've completed my first solo train journey.

CHAPTER 7

Saturday September 28th

Chloe walked into the PM Tea Shop and glanced around looking for the unmistakable tight-curled dark red hair of her friend. She soon saw her, waving from a table in the window. Crossing the room she took in the unusual decor. Against the wall directly opposite the door she saw an Edwardian glass cabinet, which housed an array of silver items and china ornaments, there was a small leather lidded box on a shelf nearby, an intricately worked metal fire screen in the hearth at the far end of the room with a large framed watercolour above it and a bronze statuette of a dancer posed from a small niche next to the big bay window. It was more like an antique shop than a cafe

Karen got up from her seat and gave her a hug.

"Happy birthday!" Chloe greeted her, handing her a

neatly wrapped parcel, before taking the seat opposite her.

"Thank you so much! " Karen carefully unwrapped the gift and was delighted with the pretty scarf in autumnal shades.

"It's beautiful! Thank you."

"I thought the colours would go so well with your hair."

"I love it."

"This place is so quirky. I've never been to anywhere quite like it," Chloe said, looking around her.

"Look at the crockery," her friend said, pointing to the delicate cup with its yellow rose bud design and gold rim. "All bone china - my plate, cup and saucer are all in the same design; yours too, but they are completely different to mine."

The waitress brought sandwiches on a silver salver which she placed in the centre of the table, this was followed by a two tier cake stand laden with large slices of cake and scones. Clotted cream was in a small blue Wedgewood dish and the raspberry jam nestled in a tiny crystal bowl each with a small silver spoon.

"I must get a photo of this," Chloe said as she took out her phone and took a snap.

The food was amazing and both girls were particularly eager to try the apple crumble cake which tasted equally as good as it looked.

English breakfast tea was served in a large cream china tea pot decorated with violets along with coordinating milk jug and a vintage double-handled silver tea strainer, compete with drip tray.

"Even the chairs are all different," Chloe noticed as she stirred her second cup of tea. "And the tables."

"The owner, Grant Andrews, deals in antiques," Karen explained. "His mother makes all the cakes for him and all the artefacts that decorate this place have a price tag on them."

Working at the tourist office meant that Karen was a font of local knowledge.

"I used to go to school with a lad of that name - I doubt if it is him though," Chloe said, looking around to see if he was in evidence. "I'll have to check their website, or look him up on Facebook and see if I recognise him."

She told Karen about her hunt for the perfect bridesmaid's dress for her sister's wedding; she wanted something in a really plain style but in a pretty colour that would suit her and the dark-haired youngster equally well.

"I think you should go for something in jade," Karen suggested. "It would suit you both. Had you thought about getting them made?"

"No. I don't know anyone who sews, and I certainly can't!" Chloe laughed.

"My mother is a dressmaker and does a lot of alterations for local people. She makes all her own clothes and always used to make mine when I was a kid. Do you want me to ask her?"

"That's certainly an idea."

"We could go to the market in Birmingham - they

have some amazing fabrics there." Karen was all fired up at the prospect.

"Well, I haven't been able to find anything I like online and there was nothing in Cheltenham either."

"That's settled then. I'll ask her and let you know."

Karen paid the bill, saying that it was her treat.

"Did you drive or come on the bus?" Karen asked as they stood to leave.

"I drove. My car's in the car park near the lock."

"That's on my way home so I'll walk with you."

They were so busy nattering as they left the building they literally bumped into a man who was passing at speed.

"I'm so sorry."

"No, it was entirely my fault. It's Chloe isn't it?"?"

Chloe hadn't actually seen her new neighbour properly so guessed. "Bob?"

"That's right." He held out his hand. "Sorry. I'm in a hurry to catch the hardware shop before it closes as I've run out of paint."

"Well, it's good to actually meet you at last." She shook his hand.

"Great - I must dash."

Chloe explained who he was after he sped off and was out of earshot.

"That was my new neighbour."

"He looks fit. Not married then?"

"No, at least I don't think so. I haven't actually met him before and I've only seen him from a distance. Mick spoke to him when he first moved in. He works for some techie firm in Amsterdam in the week and is doing up the ground floor flat at weekends. He told Mick he was planning to come back to England to live and work from home. It's a good central place for him which is also handy for the airport."

"Well, I suppose it's no worse than commuting into London."

By now they were nearly at the car park.

"Thank you so much for inviting me. I really enjoyed it."

"It was rather good, wasn't it? Thank you for coming and for my lovely scarf."

"See you soon."

By the time Chloe reached her car Karen was lost from view in the late afternoon crowd.

Driving home, Chloe wondered how Bob had got to Forest-in-the-Green. She knew he didn't have a car, and she had seen him dropped off by a taxi last Friday.

On arrival at her front door she was shocked, when she tried to turn her key, to find that it wasn't locked. She must have forgotten when she left earlier. That wasn't like her; she was always very security conscious. No one else had a key - not even Mick. She walked warily up the stairs to her flat and nervously checked every room before she could relax in the knowledge that there was nobody there. She must be more careful in future.

She was still excited at the possibility of Karen's mother making the bridesmaids' dresses and couldn't wait to phone her sister. She explained the sort of style she was thinking of and Alex thought it was a wonderful idea, and agreed that green would be a perfect colour for both her and Giles' niece Becky.

As she was talking, she wandered around the room and happened to glance out of the window as a bicycle, complete with little basket, turned into the drive. So that was how Bob had travelled to town today. He was probably used to cycling in Holland, she thought, as she watched him push the bike up to his door.

It was over an hour before she hung up, and found a text on her mobile from Mick. The coach had broken down and, although another was being sent out to pick them up, it would be very late before they got home. She sent a message back saying she would miss him but would see him tomorrow morning.

At a loose end, she picked up her iPad and scrolled through Facebook to see what her friends were doing tonight. She noticed a friend request from a Linda Simmonds and clicked on the avatar, which was of a cute kitten, to get more information, as she didn't recognise the name. It seemed that they had gone to the same school. She remembered a Linda Hughes and realised that, like many of her friends, she must now be married, so clicked to accept, then sent a message, "Are you Linda Hughes?" just to make sure.

She resumed scrolling down her news feed to find that someone was selling a set of multi- coloured shot glasses, a cat had gone missing from a nearby street and Sally from work was at a Chinese buffet with the most enormous plate of food in front of her.

Messenger pinged and there was a reply from her old classmate. "Yes, It's me. How are you?"

They chatted on Messenger for a while, catching up with how their lives had changed since their days at the comprehensive.

Remembering the photo she had taken earlier of the sumptuous afternoon tea, she uploaded it and tagged Karen in before grabbing her sci-fi novel and heading for bed.

CHAPTER 8

Thursday October 10th

Mick rolled over to turn off the alarm and shivered as he climbed out of bed. He might have to think about turning on the heating. His parents had left yesterday for a week in sunny Mallorca, so it was up to him to fend for himself for a few days. He had a quick shower and shave before wandering into the kitchen, and while he waited for the kettle to boil he poured himself a large helping of cereal.

Today he had to fit a couple of new radiators in a beautiful detached house in The Chestnuts, a small cul-de-sac on the edge of town; the sort of house he would love to own one day. Somewhere with a bit of character - not like the modern boxes on the new development, which all looked the same. At least living with his parents he was able to save well and by the time he was ready to fly the nest he would have a good deposit to put down.

After lacing his work boots he made a list of the items he would need to pick up from his little lock-up unit. He took a bottle of water from the fridge along with the sandwiches he'd made last night, put them into his canvas lunch bag and set off to the car park at the rear of the house. The van could do with a wash, he thought as he rounded the corner.

"Oh, great." Someone had scrawled something in the grime across the back doors. When he got closer he was able to read what was written there.

"STAY AWAY FROM HER - SHE'S MINE"

He had been expecting it to say something more along the lines of 'Wash Me', or some rude comment, so he was rather taken aback. Who could have written it - and who was the 'she' it referred to?

He found an old rag in the van and, using some of his bottled water, he managed to wipe off the message, then sat for a while, thinking. At most premises where he worked there was usually only the woman of the house there. He would often be offered a drink and then they would stay out of his way, though there was always the odd one who wanted to follow him round talking and generally keeping an eye on him in case he ran off with the family jewels. This made absolutely no sense at all; with a gorgeous girlfriend like Chloe he didn't need to look elsewhere.

He started up the motor and drove to the lock-up to load up the necessary items. He had to move a box of tiles that had been left over from a job a couple of weeks ago; he had meant to take them back to the wholesaler, and would have to do so soon if he wanted to get his money back. He'd been glad to finish that bathroom refit. He'd only seen the husband the one time, when he went to price up the job. Now he remembered the bored housewife had been a bit too friendly for his liking. Middle aged but in good shape, she had moaned about her husband always being away on business while showing rather too much leg when she sat on the edge of the bath. She may have said something to her husband to give him the wrong idea, or maybe one of the neighbours had noticed his van had been outside for days while her husband was away. She kept finding more things she wanted him to do - extras that she wanted fitting. It had made him late starting his next project. She hadn't liked the original bathroom cabinet either and he was still waiting for the new one to arrive so that he could get it fitted and send in the bill. He was looking forward to going back there less than ever now.

"No," he said out loud, and shook his head as if to erase the thought. It was more likely to be one of the neighbours having a laugh at his expense; one of the chaps from the pub or some young lads with nothing better to do.

By the time he was ringing the bell next to the beautiful solid oak door at Five, The Chestnuts, it had been forgotten.

CHAPTER 9

Wednesday October 16th

Wednesday morning was Brenda Hartley's day off from her job at the Post Office. She had just come in from pegging the washing onto the line when her friend knocked at the door. She dragged a comb quickly through her short, greying hair before opening up.

"Come on in, Di. It looks like being a nice day."

"It's meant to stay like this for a few days," her friend commented, glancing up at the cloudless blue sky before crossing the threshold.

"Oh, I do hope so. Everyone is so much happier when the sun shines. It makes the working day go quicker when the customers are smiling." Brenda ushered Diane into the living room, which still smelt of the lavender furniture polish she had used to give the oak sideboard a good shine.

"I've brought some chocolate digestive biscuits this morning," Di said, retrieving the packet from her shopping bag and handing it over.

"Ooh, lovely, anyone would think it was a celebration."

"Well it is, sort of. I'll tell you all about it when you sit down."

Brenda nipped into the kitchen and was soon back with two lattes, which her pod coffee machine had quickly produced, along with a couple of dainty china plates for the biscuits.

"Well?" she asked as she set the wooden tray down onto the small coffee table.

Diane handed her an envelope. "Have a look and see."

"An invitation? A wedding. Oh how wonderful!"

"Yes, my little boy is getting married," Diane told her proudly.

Brenda read. "Mr and Mrs Edward Thornby request the pleasure...ooh, Alexandra - what a lovely name. And that's a very posh place. I'll have to buy a new frock to be seen there."

"It is rather nice - set in lovely grounds."

"It seems like yesterday when we first met at the school gates, waiting for our boys to come bounding out," Brenda sighed.

"It's thirty years, Bren. Where has the time gone?"

"Gosh knows."

"You will come won't you - and Robin too?" Di asked as she dunked a second biscuit into her drink.

"Of course we will. It seems such a shame the boys drifted apart when they went to different senior schools."

"Different interests, different lives. It was bound to happen."

"I don't think Robin will ever get married."

"Never say never. He just hasn't found the right girl."

"He won't find anyone if he never goes out. Sometimes I wonder if he might be gay - he has never had a girlfriend, as far as I know. He studied hard at university and now his career is his life."

"Poor lad," her friend commiserated.

"I blame myself. He started eating for comfort when he lost his dad, and before I knew it the weight had just piled on him."

"He has become such a lovely man though. You must be so proud of him. The kiddies love him; he's such a good teacher."

Diane's eldest, Christine, had school-aged children who had been in his class.

"He does put his heart and soul into his job. Every night after dinner he goes straight upstairs to his room to prepare the work for the following day. I hardly see anything of him."

"Well, surely he goes out sometime. At the weekends?"

"Ever since he saw a programme on television about endangered species, he has been obsessed with making money to help them. He is planning to walk the full length of the country from Land's End to John O'Groats next summer. Every Friday he packs up the car and leaves straight from work to go off to the countryside where he spends the weekend sleeping in a tent and walking to get fit enough for the task."

"It's so sad that so many animal species are decreasing in number. I'll sponsor him if you have a form. "

"He hasn't got one yet, but I'll let you know when he does. "

"He may set up a Just Giving page instead - apparently it's a lot easier."

"I'll suggest that to him."

"How's your sister?" Diane remembered that her friend had been staying with her sister for the past few days to care for her when she came out of hospital after her hysterectomy.

"She's doing really well, although she's got to take it easy for a whole month. She can't do any heavy lifting or even get the vacuum cleaner out. Fred will have to do that at the weekends."

"It won't hurt him."

"He's actually quite helpful about the house."

"They've got a prize bingo at the community centre on the sixth of November, in aid of the local drama group. Do you want to come?" Di asked. "They are going to have some good prizes."

"That sounds like fun. I haven't been for years. Jamie and I used to always go to the Christmas one at the football club before Robin came along. I got the star prize of a fantastic hamper the last time we went."

The two ladies carried on talking for a good hour before Diane looked at the ornate carriage clock on the sideboard and told her friend she needed to get off. Her book was due back to the library and she didn't want to get a fine.

They said their goodbyes and agreed to the same time next week at Diane's home.

CHAPTER 10

Thursday October 31st

It was warm for the end of October and it had been busy at the farm with a lot of Halloween themed activities and many half-term visitors to enjoy them as they made the most of the sunshine. There were several entrants for the fancy dress competition each day and children had enjoyed a treasure hunt. Witches' brew and spider-web cup cakes were on offer, and this morning Chloe, suitably dressed as a witch, had enjoyed helping children to make grotesque lanterns out of pumpkins.

She had finished her packed lunch in her cubby-hole office and was flicking through her social media accounts. She 'liked' a few photos on Instagram before turning her attention to Facebook. One post on the local newspaper site caught her eye: 'A man has been discovered this morning, injured and unconscious, in the village of Bulls Cross. Police are at the scene and it is not yet known how he came by his injuries.'

She sent Mick a text asking him if he had heard anything about it, threw her crisp packet into the bin then made her way to the kiosk so that her colleague Sally could go for her lunch. She enjoyed being able to interact with the various people who came through the turnstile.

When she returned to her office she checked her mobile but there were no messages. She made a start on the animal feed order, regularly staring out of the window at the beautiful countryside, bathed in sunshine and in all its autumn glory. The beeches were looking particularly stunning with their golden leaves and she thought that maybe she'd suggest to Mick that they go to an arboretum on Sunday – Westonbirt perhaps. They had thought of taking a picnic there in the summer but hadn't got round to it, and this would be the ideal time to catch the trees at their best.

Afternoons were shorter now since the clocks went back last weekend and she was locking up at four thirty. On her way home she mulled over what she would eat tonight before her weekly badminton game at the sports hall. Pasta would be quick and easy and there was a piece of chorizo in the fridge that needed to be used up. She enjoyed cooking but rarely had the time and anyway there didn't seem much point in cooking a proper meal for one.

As she pulled up outside the house she was surprised

to see Pete's car parked there. She reached over to grab her handbag and lunch box as Pete dashed round to open her door for her.

"Hi, Pete, what are you doing here?" Chloe smiled, and then noticed the look on his face.

"It's Mick - he's been in an accident."

The blood drained from Chloe's face. "What happened? Is he all right?"

"He's alive and he's been taken to hospital, but he is still unconscious."

"Which hospital?"

"Queen Elizabeth."

"I must go and see him." She made to get back into her car, throwing her bag and box back in but Pete grabbed her shoulder to stop her.

"His parents are there at the moment." He spoke slowly and calmly. "They're only allowing next of kin. His mother phoned me and asked me to let you know as she had no way of contacting you herself."

"What happened?" Chloe asked again.

"A neighbour found him early this morning in the lane that leads to the residential car park. It looks like he was knocked down by a vehicle of some sort. The police have been there all day."

"How could anyone just leave him there?" Chloe slumped against the bonnet of her car. "How could anyone be so cruel?"

"Come on, Chloe," Pete urged her. "Let's go indoors and I'll make you a drink."

Chloe allowed him to take her arm and lead her to

her door, but still in shock, she struggled with the lock.

Pete held his hand out for the keys. "Give them to me."

Chloe led the way up to her living room. Pete had never been to her flat before but the kitchen door was open so he went straight in and soon found everything to make a strong, sweet coffee.

"I still can't believe this," she said as he put the drink beside her. "I read about it on the net this morning but never thought for one minute that it would be Mick. I thought that some old boy had fallen and injured himself on his way home from the pub."

She was clearly upset, but to Pete's relief she hadn't burst into tears. He wasn't any good with dealing with emotions. He was worried about his mate too, and didn't know what to do, especially as he needed to get home. He and Karen were taking a birthday present to his father this evening and his mother had made a cake specially.

Chloe could see that he was feeling awkward.

"Thanks so much for coming to let me know. I'll be okay," she told him as she picked up her handbag and searched for a pen and notebook. "I'm going to ring the hospital and see what I can find out. Here's my mobile number. Could you pass it on to Mick's mum? Please let me know if you hear anything."

Pete took the slip of paper and promised that he would. He gave her a quick, awkward hug.

"Call me if you need me, or Karen," he urged her. "I know she'll come over at any time."

"Thanks, Pete. I'll be fine, honestly."

Once she had locked the door, she looked up the phone number for the hospital and dialled it on the house phone. It was a useless exercise as they said they could not divulge any information. She was glad that she had given Pete her mobile number as hopefully he would be in touch.

She shivered. The flat was cold as the heating had only just started up and would take a time to warm through. She would have to alter the timer so it would come on earlier. It had always been so cosy to come home to when Mrs Bridges had been living downstairs. Heat had risen from the large solid fuel range in her kitchen where school dinners had been prepared in the past. Chloe would often be met by a wonderful aroma of cooking when she arrived home. She doubted her new neighbour would bother to light it at weekends, although she would be happy to be proved wrong.

Feeling lost, she wondered whether to go to badminton tonight or not, and decided that it would be better to stay put in case anyone rang. Although she wasn't hungry she knew she should eat. Soup would help to ward off the cold, she decided, and opened a tin of oxtail, which had been left in the cupboard since last winter. As she watched the bowl go round and round in the microwave she willed Mick to wake up and be okay.

CHAPTER 11

Saturday November 2nd

Chloe decided to go for her usual run this morning. She was sick of her own company and needed to get out. Taking the day off work yesterday hadn't been a good idea; she hadn't been able to settle and had spent the day fretting.

Mrs Benfield had called the previous night to let Chloe know that although Mick was still unconscious, they had been able to operate on his broken leg. They had done a brain scan and were confident that he would soon be back with them. Chloe had asked if she could visit him but she was told that she would not be allowed yet, but Mrs Benfield would keep her informed and would let her know just as soon as she could.

As she arrived at the starting point she saw Jeremy and, although she was sure that he had seen her, he made no attempt to come over to speak to her. He had probably heard about what had happened to Mick and didn't know what to say. He was a strange guy, and she believed he was actually quite shy.

The run was therapeutic. It was so good to be out in the fresh air; she felt really invigorated as she pounded around the course and was glad she had come.

It was necessary to call by the supermarket on her way home and again she found it hard to concentrate. Wandering aimlessly around the store she put a packet of Mick's favourite biscuits into the trolley without realising it, and was going to put them back on the shelf, then decided that she could take them to the hospital with her when he came round and was able to enjoy them. Hospital food could leave a lot to be desired.

One road on the route home was closed due to a burst water main, and it took longer than usual to negotiate the alternative, narrow country lanes. As she finally pulled into the drive Bob was just leaving his flat and met her halfway as she walked to her door.

"Can I help you with those?" he offered, nodding to her shopping bags.

"That would be kind of you." She handed over the heaviest of the bags. "I bought rather more than I meant to."

"Your boyfriend gone to football?"

"No, he's in hospital," she told him and went on to explain what had happened as they walked together to her flat.

"That's really dreadful," he said as he put the bag down on the landing. "Is there anything I can do? Anything you need? I'll be here until first thing Monday."

"I don't think so - but thank you," she answered as he turned to leave.

"I was hoping I'd see you, actually," he said, looking back. "Could you keep an eye on my flat? I won't be able to get over for a few weeks. Push any fliers through, that sort of thing."

"Yes, of course."

Chloe thought she should perhaps have offered him a coffee as she started to fill the fridge with food and wine, but she wasn't really in the mood to make small talk with someone who was little more than a stranger.

She made herself a mug of instant black coffee and settled down with a packet of custard creams to check her mobile. There was a missed call and someone had left her a message. As she went through the steps to retrieve it she hoped that it would be good news about Mick. It was neither Mrs Benfield nor Pete but a DI Shaun Willis, who asked her to ring him back as he needed to speak to her. Worried, she quickly dialled the mobile number.

"DI Willis."

"Hello, this is Chloe Thornby. You asked me to ring you?"

"Ah yes, I'd like to talk to you about your boyfriend's accident. Would it be okay to come over now?"

"Yes, I'm at home and haven't any plans to go

anywhere this afternoon."

He asked for her address and checked the postcode for his satnav.

"I'll be with you in about forty five minutes."

"Okay." He had given no clue as to why he wanted to speak to her, and her mind churned with the possibilities.

She looked around at the mess her living room was in and decided that she ought to give it a quick tidy before the detective arrived. She gathered up the open mail on the coffee table and stuffed it into a drawer, took the empty coffee mug into the kitchen and put it into the sink. The washing, which she had draped over the radiator to dry days ago, was quickly removed and taken through to the bedroom to be put away later.

Still in her running gear, she glanced quickly at her watch; there was just enough time for a quick shower and change. As she zipped up her jeans she heard the doorbell ring. She looked in the bathroom mirror and gave her hair a quick brush before bounding down the stairs to answer it.

She found a tall, dark, middle-aged man waiting for her.

"Miss Thornby?"

"Yes."

He held out his ID. "DI Willis."

Although she was expecting him, she took it and scrutinised it carefully before handing it back.

"You had better come in."

Chloe noticed a whiff of aftershave as she closed the

door behind them.

When they reached the landing she showed him into the living room and gestured for him to take the armchair by the fireplace, where a small gas fire glowed. She sat on the end of the sofa at an angle to him.

"I really can't think why you want to speak to me," she said.

"We have reason to believe that Michael was knocked down deliberately, and not by accident as originally thought."

Chloe was visibly shocked and stared open-mouthed at him.

"I need to ask you a few questions."

Chloe nodded, still lost for words.

"Can you tell me what time Michael left you on Wednesday evening?"

"It was about eleven o'clock."

"What did you do after he had left?"

"I locked the door and went straight to bed."

"Did you hear anything strange - another car start up, maybe?"

"No, but I was tired and went to sleep very quickly."

"Can you think of anyone who would wish him harm?"

"Of course not! Everybody loves him. He is such a wonderful caring person - how could anyone want to hurt him?"

"How long have you known him?"

"Almost six months."

"Did he tell you that someone wrote a warning on his van a few weeks ago?"

"No. What sort of warning?"

"He told his mother that he thought it might be a client thinking he was getting too friendly with his wife."

"He never said anything to me," Chloe replied.

"He probably didn't want to worry you," Willis soothed before asking, "Do you have any ex-boyfriends that could be jealous?"

"I moved here when my fiancé died. A new job, a new home and a new start. I've lived here for three years now and, until I met Mick, I hadn't been interested in dating."

"I am so sorry to hear of your loss. How did your fiancé die?"

"He had a heart condition they didn't know about and collapsed on the rugby pitch. At least he was doing something he loved," she replied with tears in her eyes.

"I think that's all for now." Willis got up and closed his notebook. "If you think of anyone at all who may have held a grudge or could have been responsible, ring me straight away."

He handed her his card and made his way to the top of the stairs as she followed, clearly upset.

"This is all just so wrong! I can't think of anyone who would do such a thing to Mick. He's such a nice guy."

"Thanks for your time, Miss Thornby."

Chloe locked the door behind him and went back to make another coffee as the original one had got cold. She thought better of it and helped herself to a large glass of wine and was about to take a good swig when the doorbell rang again.

She found DI Willis back on her doorstep.

"Does anyone live in the ground floor flat?" he asked.

"Yes - but he was just leaving for a walk round the area when I arrived home from the supermarket."

"I could do with talking to him. He may have heard something on Wednesday night."

"Well, I can help you there. He lives in Amsterdam in the week and is only here at weekends so he wouldn't have been here then."

Willis looked around, noting that the house stood in its own grounds, there were only fields on the other side of the road and the village church amid its gravestones over the red-brick wall. He thanked her and headed for his car.

CHAPTER 12

Monday November 4th

After a restless weekend at home Chloe was more than ready to get back to work. She hadn't heard anything from Mrs Benfield and didn't want to bother her. She had Pete's number but he had promised to let her know if there was any news.

On leaving the house she almost tripped over a large bouquet of flowers on her doorstep. She picked them up to see who they were from but there was no card on them and no indication of who had delivered them. Nobody ever sent her flowers so they must have been delivered to the wrong address; there was no other explanation. She quickly took them upstairs and hurriedly plonked them in the kitchen sink with some water. Someone might come and claim them but in the meantime she needed to keep them hydrated.

Driving to work, her mind was free to wander back to Mick and what the detective had said. Surely nobody could have wanted to harm him. Overwhelmed by a mixture of emotions she was near to tears when she parked up in the yard. Her boss, James, was just leaving the farmhouse when she arrived and strode over to meet her.

"Are you sure you should be here?" he asked kindly.

"Yes. I can't visit Mick. There's nothing I can do, so I might as well be at work," she sniffed. "It will help take my mind off everything."

"Well, I have plenty to keep you busy here. Mrs Smith from the village called me yesterday evening, asking if we would be organising 'Christmas Carols in the Stable' again. She said how much everyone had enjoyed it last year."

Chloe had been in her element co-ordinating the event and had been thrilled that it was such a success. She remembered the dozens of night lights along the edge of the path which led the way to the stable in the main yard. There had been mulled wine for the adults and hot chocolate for the children, and Neddy the donkey had safely delivered James' daughter to the event.

"I can design some posters and get in touch with the school to ask if they would like to do a couple of carols for us again," she suggested as they walked together to the office.

"Mrs Smith said that the WI would like to do something, so speak to her too," her boss advised.

It was late morning when Mrs Benfield rang Chloe to tell her that Mick had regained consciousness. She was on her way home to have something to eat before going back to visit him later and asked if Chloe would like to go and see him this evening.

"Oh, yes! Thank you, I'd really like that."

"There's something I need to warn you..."

"I can't hear you - you're breaking up." Chloe shouted.

The line went dead.

Chloe tried to ring her back but it went straight through to voice mail.

She must be in a bad service area, Chloe thought as she went back to her computer. At long last she would be able to see Mick. His mother probably wanted to warn her what a mess he was in as he was no doubt covered in cuts and bruises, but all that mattered was that he was alive.

The hospital visiting started at seven o'clock so she had time to grab a sandwich before leaving and decided to put on a mustard yellow jumper that she had bought recently. She went to the drawer but couldn't find it. She was sure she had put it there. She remembered wearing it the once for a short time and had put it away to wear another day before putting it in the wash. She swiftly rummaged through all the drawers but she couldn't find it. Time was running out, so she had no choice but to wear another one instead.

It took ages to find a parking space, and then she had

to pay for a ticket at the machine. She didn't know which ward Mick was on so called at reception on her way in and was told he was in a side ward in the North block. It was 7.15 by the time she walked nervously through the doors and began to search the faces as she passed. She found him propped up in a bed near the end.

"Hello, sweetheart." She went to kiss him, but he looked shocked and turned away.

"What's wrong? I'm sorry I couldn't get here any earlier, but they wouldn't let me."

"Who are you?" he asked.

"Don't be silly, of course you know me," she laughed.

His blank look showed her that he didn't. Something was definitely wrong.

Stunned, Chloe turned and almost walked into a nurse. She told her what had happened. Introducing herself as the ward sister, the woman took her to an office and invited her to sit down. She explained that her patient had lost sections of his memory.

"How long have you known Michael?" the nurse asked.

"Almost six months."

"We know that he recognised his parents this afternoon straight away but appears to remember nothing about the accident. It seems that his amnesia goes back to a point some time before it happened," she explained. "It can take anything from a few days to some months or much longer to regain those memories, and some he may never get back."

"What should I do?" asked Chloe, close to tears.

"Go back and calmly tell him who you are and a little about yourself. Carry on visiting him each day and talk to him about things you have done together which may help trigger his memory of you."

"Okay," Chloe replied, and taking a deep breath walked back down the ward.

"Hello," she said, pulling up a chair. "I'm Chloe Thornby and I'm your girlfriend."

CHAPTER 13

Thursday November 14th

Chloe scampered downstairs in a cheerful mood. Mick had been discharged from hospital yesterday, and she was looking forward to planning the decorations for this year's Christmas event at the farm. When she reached the front door there was an envelope on the doormat. Her name was hand-written on the front in a way that suggested the writer had used a ruler to write along as the bottom of the letters were flat and the word very straight. She didn't recognise the handwriting so slowly slid her thumb under the flap and pulled out a single sheet of A4 paper carrying a typed message.

"You looked beautiful in that green sweater last night."

She had spent the evening with Mick yesterday and had indeed worn her green jumper, which she knew to be Mick's favourite. He must have asked someone to pop it through her door because he wouldn't be seeing her tonight. What a lovely thought.

It had been over a week since Mick had regained consciousness and Chloe had been at his side every evening since. He still didn't remember her but they were able to talk easily together, and he seemed happy getting to know her all over again. His parents were a homely couple and had made her feel very welcome.

Pete was taking Mick to darts at the Bull's Head tonight; although he wouldn't be able to play, at least it would get him out of the house for a while. Chloe would go to badminton club and start to bring some normality back into her life too. It would be good for them to have a break from each other as they used to: they didn't need to see each other every day.

She arrived at work with a spring in her step. The golden morning light brightened up everything from the hedgerows to the big Dutch barn where the cattle were busy munching hay from the long wooden trough.

While she waited for her computer to warm up, she sent Mick a quick text to thank him for the note. Still smiling she started to look at a few sites where she might get some festive lights which she could string along the fence each side of the short drive.

James came dashing in. "The pigs have got out. They're in the vegetable patch, " he yelled. "Can you come and help round them up?"

He ran out again leaving Chloe to pull on her coat and wellingtons before rushing after him. James, his wife Dawn and a couple of others were already running around trying to herd Clover and her piglets towards the garden gate when she joined them.

"Quick - stand by the flower border and catch any piglets that come your way," James yelled at Chloe as he tried to coax the sow away from his carrots with the aid of a piece of chipboard.

"Got one!" shouted Dawn.

"Put it in the old sty." Geoff, the new pig man, hollered as he too caught an errant young pig.

Just as they returned James tripped over and fell headlong into the compost heap. The pig took the opportunity to race at full pelt into the orchard. James slowly got up but had some potato peel adorning his unruly hair. Chloe burst out laughing at the sight and was soon joined by Dawn, while James stomped off after Clover with no idea what all the hilarity was about.

The final two piglets were caught and James finally steered the greedy sow into the old secure sty with her young for the time being. Thankfully they hadn't caused too much damage, although the sprouts had taken a direct hit from the ever hungry mother.

Geoff had reported yesterday that he wasn't happy with the catch on the pen as it had become difficult to close properly. Someone would have to go to the ironmongers in town as a matter of urgency.

"I can do that," Chloe said. "I could look for some lights for the Christmas display while I'm out."

"That would be a great help," James said. "I've got the AI man coming, and I really need to be here to oversee the insemination of the heifers."

It was a short distance into town and she very soon purchased a strong new fastener for the pen, then continued to Paul's Plants. She found a magnificent large reindeer, which she thought would look fantastic at the entrance of the farm with his red nose shining like a beacon, but decided that James' eyes would water at the price, so settled for two long rope lights, which she could ask Mick's friend Pete, an electrician, to set up for her. Paul helped her load them into her little car and promised to deliver a six foot Christmas tree nearer the date. Chloe thanked him and headed back to the farm, full of early festive cheer.

She handed the catch to Geoff. "I'll fit that right away," he said. "Once pigs know the way out, there's no stopping them. Right little escape artists, they are."

Chloe laughed, and headed back into her office. She checked her mobile while she decided what to do next. There was a message from Mick, and she eagerly opened it.

"What note?"

She gasped and held on to the edge of her desk. She had been so certain it had been from him. If it wasn't, then who was it from? An awful thought struck her as she realised that whoever it was must have been close enough to see what she was wearing. It had been well lit along the route she had taken from the street where there were no parking restrictions, but she couldn't remember seeing anyone. She had been in a bit of a hurry because she hadn't taken a coat and it was colder than she had thought. Perhaps someone had followed her. Maybe she should tell the police? No; they wouldn't be interested. It wasn't as if she had been threatened in any way.

So why did she feel so uneasy?

CHAPTER 14

Friday November 15th

It was now two months since Paula had started her studies at Bristol University. She had plenty of time for her course work in the evenings as she hadn't really made any friends. The other freshers she shared with only seemed to be there to enjoy the freedom of student life, when she'd told them she wasn't interested in going out drinking every night they soon stopped including her in their plans. Her house mates had already been there a year and had their own social network. She was lonely, and decided to go home for the weekend even though she really couldn't afford the train fare. Her mother had been thrilled when she had phoned saying that she would like to visit.

The train today was already quite full but I was able to

find a seat next to a businessman, who was busy tapping away on his laptop. A couple were sitting on the other side of the table arguing about something. On the opposite side of the carriage four lads were playing cards, and each had a pack of beer which had already been started. I read a magazine to pass the time.

The other passengers changed at each station and I was glad to see the back of the couple opposite when they got up to leave at Cheltenham Spa. Someone took their seat and when I glanced up I was pleasantly surprised to be looking straight into the blue eyes of the handsome man I had seen the last time I travelled home. I know I was blushing as my face was red hot when he smiled at me. It was obvious that he recognised me from before but he didn't speak and there was no way I was going to strike up a conversation. I wonder who he is and where he was going to.

CHAPTER 15

Saturday November 16th

Chloe would have forgotten about meeting up with Karen today if she hadn't received a text from her last night. It had all been arranged before Mick's accident and she hadn't given her sister's wedding much thought since. As she waited at the bus stop she felt vulnerable, wondering if someone was watching her right now. She had been on edge ever since she had found out that Mick hadn't sent the note. It could have been a perfectly innocent communication from a secret admirer thinking she was no longer with Mick, not having seen her with him lately, but she wasn't convinced. It didn't feel quite right.

The bus was late and she was cold and miserable when it finally arrived. She was glad to find a seat well away from the door, where she would get the most benefit from the heater. It felt safe to be in the company of others. After three stops her friend boarded the bus and made straight for the seat beside her, sitting down heavily as the bus pulled away with a jerk and made her lose her balance.

"It's so good to see you," Chloe told her.

"How are you? How's Mick? It must be so hard waiting for him to remember you."

"I'll be glad when he does. It's just the past six to eight months he is missing, and it's like starting all over, except that I already know him but he's getting to know me afresh. They think he will remember eventually, but maybe not the actual accident."

The bus was full by the time it reached the city so it took quite a while before they were out in the crisp November air. They wandered through the Bullring outdoor market, where stalls were full of a wonderful selection of fruit and vegetables, some of which Chloe had never seen before. From there they made their way to the indoor Rag Market, a huge building where mini-shops were selling everything from meat to household goods. A large section housed fabrics and there were so many rolls of material in every type, pattern and colour imaginable that they didn't know where to start. There were sequins, lace, buttons and all manner of trimmings too.

Karen pointed out some jewel-like taffetas in purple, blue and red. "Lovely shades," she murmured, "but perhaps not for you."

"They are pretty but they wouldn't suit me," Chloe

agreed as they passed a stall piled high with poly-cotton prints. "The wedding's at the end of May, so it could be quite warm. We won't want anything too heavy."

Further on they found some beautiful brocade fabrics, one in teal green with a gold pattern which Chloe thought was perfect. The pretty Asian woman told them that it was silk for making into saris, and asked them what they intended to use it for. Chloe showed her the pattern which she and Karen's mother had chosen, and the woman shook her head. She took the roll from the shelf and showed them that the gold work was only along the edges; it would be lost if it was cut into a dress. Chloe was crestfallen, but she had to agree that it wasn't appropriate. "Right idea, though," she told Karen. "We're getting closer."

The girls carried on browsing and finally decided on an emerald satin. When the stallholder saw the pattern, he suggested a gold brocade ribbon which could be used as a trimming.

"This is going to be lovely!" Chloe exclaimed as they left carrying a carrier bag each as the necessary material for each dress had been cut separately so that they could share the weight between them.

"Mum can't wait to get started. She wants plenty of time to get them made and fitting perfectly for the big day," Karen told her. "In fact, she said this morning that if we're in good time this afternoon she would like to get you measured up."

They both had other shopping to do in the Bullring but they would be back in Forest-in-the-Green after lunch, which would work out very well.

There were plenty of places to eat in the area around the shopping centre and they opted for a restaurant where they had some good vegetarian and vegan options for Karen. It was already quite busy when they arrived but the helpful waitress found them a table near the window. As they settled in, Karen noticed that her friend was frowning. "What's up?"

"Oh, nothing." She had caught a man on the next table watching them and had started thinking about the mystery note. Somehow the idea of putting her anxieties into words felt as if it would give them credence. She summoned up a smile, squeezing her friend's arm to reassure her. "Just thinking of Mick and wondering how long it will be until he remembers me again."

"Talking of memories," Karen said, "Grant Andrews came into the TIC the other day to leave some leaflets for his afternoon teas. He was telling me that he'd moved here from Gloucestershire. I remembered your remark that you went to school with someone with the same name so I asked him whereabouts in the county. When he said he was from near Cheltenham I told him that you thought you went to school with him. I told him your name and he remembered you - said to tell you he'd love to catch up with you some time."

"Grant was in the year above me, and quite popular with the girls, but not really my type," Chloe said.

"He's certainly nothing like Mick, that's for sure," Karen smiled. "He gave me a voucher for a cream tea for two so maybe we could go and make use of that sometime. It would be good to meet up on Saturdays when the boys are at footie."

"I'd like that. Do you fancy going to the cinema next week?"

"That's a terrific idea. I never get to go these days as Pete prefers to watch DVDs at home. What sort of film would you prefer?"

"Nothing heavy - a comedy of some sort."

"That sounds like a plan. We'll have a look to see what's on when we get to Mum's."

As they were gathering their shopping to leave, Chloe noticed the large form of Geoff the pig man, sitting facing them from a table by the wall. He smiled and acknowledged her with a slight nod of the head. She discreetly waved back.

Karen raised her eyebrows curiously.

"Just a guy from work," Chloe told her.

CHAPTER 16

Wednesday November 20th

Diane had just got home from the school run. Her daughter, Christine, had dropped the kiddies off early this morning as she had a scan appointment at the hospital. This house always seemed such a mess, she thought, as she tidied away the toys. What must Brenda think when hers was always so sparkling and tidy? "Well, my home is lived in," she consoled herself out loud as she wandered through to the kitchen She looked around and groaned; there were degrees of 'lived in', some more acceptable than others. There always seemed to be washing up to be done. If only she had a dishwasher! She rolled up her sleeves to make a start but had hardly made any headway when her friend arrived.

"Come on in, love." She opened the door wide and

stood back, drying her hands on her floral apron.

Brenda made her way straight to the living room and sat down, as she always did, in the chair by the window. The sun was shining and cast a prism of colour on the opposite wall as it caught the small crystal vase Diane kept on the windowsill. Photos of her ever-growing family adorned all surfaces from the sideboard to the little nest of tables next to Diane's favourite chair. Brenda always liked coming here; it was so cosy.

Diane bustled in with two mugs and a packet of Rich Tea which she placed on the low coffee table in front of Brenda

"Sorry I haven't got anything more exciting," she pointed at the biscuits, "but I put the bourbons in the little ones' lunch boxes."

"I'm trying to lose weight, actually, and I'm pretty sure they don't have too many calories."

"What do you want to lose weight for?" her plump friend asked.

"Well, it's not much more than a month until Christmas and I've decided to treat Robin to a week away. He works so hard, and deserves something special. With only the two of us it's hardly worth cooking a proper Christmas dinner every year, so I decided to let someone else do it instead."

"That's a wonderful idea! Where are you taking him?"

"We're having an all-inclusive break in Madeira, leaving on Saturday the 21st," Brenda told her excitedly. "I've booked a taxi so he won't even have to drive to the airport."

"Wow! You little globe trotter, you. Have you told him yet?"

"No - I'll tell him nearer the time."

"You'll love it. I've heard it's very pretty there. A chance to unwind and a good rest for you both," Di said, although she was feeling a little bit jealous.

"What with one thing and another I hardly get chance to have a proper conversation with him these days, although he has agreed with me that it's too cold now for him to be out camping at the weekends. He's going to just go hiking in the daytime nearer to home. It'll be a chance to actually spend some quality time with him."

"You'll be able to walk together when you're away," Di said. "Some friends went there on a walking holiday and said the views were absolutely stunning."

"Maybe, but he gets a bit frustrated with me because I'm rather slower than him."

"He must be getting really fit now."

"How are the wedding plans going?"

"Giles doesn't say a lot. We're all meant to be meeting up after Christmas, so I'll know more after that. Alex's parents live in Andoversford so it'll probably be somewhere in town. By then I hope they'll have decided on a colour scheme so her mother and I will know what to avoid wearing. Afterwards, perhaps you'll be able to come shopping and help me choose an outfit. Bill hasn't got a clue and I'd like an honest opinion."

"I would love to. Maybe I can find something at the

same time."

"We could catch the train to Birmingham and make a day of it."

"That sounds like a very good idea. I haven't been for years and I've heard they have some very good shops there."

CHAPTER 17

Saturday November 23rd

It had been a cold, wet and windy run in the park this morning and, although she was feeling the benefits of the exercise in the fresh air, Chloe was glad to get back in her car, only to find that someone had put a flyer under the windscreen wiper. She sighed, clambered out to remove it and threw it onto the passenger seat to look at later. She was soaked, the windows were already beginning to steam up and all she wanted to do right now was get home to a warm shower and some dry clothes.

She had just got into the shower when the house phone started to ring. Blow that, she thought; she would dial 1471 and ring them back later. Very few people called her on the house phone and she hoped it wasn't Karen cancelling. She was really looking forward to their trip out.

Warmed and dressed, Chloe discovered that the caller had not left their number. "Probably some sales rubbish," she muttered as she went through to the kitchen to get a drink. She'd received a lot of those calls recently where there was no one there when she answered. Not that she wanted to talk to anyone about double glazing, or the accident she hadn't had, and she knew that they were mostly computer-generated, but it was still bloody annoying all the same. At least it wasn't a heavy breather.

She took a chocolate biscuit and her coffee to the living room. She had a few minutes to look online for a Christmas gift for Mick, thinking of something like a warm jumper for him. As was often the case, she lost track of the time, and suddenly realised that she needed to leave very soon. Karen was expecting her to be there at midday so she hastily unhooked her coat from the back of the door and ran out to her car.

The traffic was bad as she drove to town, which made her even later, so she wasn't surprised to find her friend anxiously waiting in the doorway.

"Sorry, the traffic was really awful," she said as Karen struggled with her seatbelt.

"I heard on the radio that there's been an accident on the motorway and everything's been diverted this way," Karen said.

"It's a good job we're going in the opposite direction then, or we'd be late for the cinema. I do love any film with Hugh Grant in it."

"So do I. It will be so good to have a laugh, and he's easy on the eye, too," she added with a grin.

At the car park, Karen handed her some change for the ticket machine. Chloe was grateful to find that she had the correct coins as she didn't like having to use her debit card on these machines. Returning to place the ticket on the dashboard, she saw her friend reading the flyer from this morning, which she had forgotten all about.

"What's this?" Karen asked.

"Well, you should know; you've been reading it."

Karen thrust the piece of paper into Chloe's hand. 'You looked as beautiful as ever in your running gear,' it said. It was the same straight writing as before.

Chloe went cold as she looked at her friend's surprised expression.

"It's not what you think," she stuttered as she dropped the ticket and had to bend to fish it out from under the pedals.

"Who's it from?" Karen asked, noticing that Chloe's hand was shaking.

"I don't know. It was under my windscreen wiper when I got back to the car at the park this morning. I thought it was a flyer because I've had them before advertising trainers or a local charity run."

"Come on, we'll go and get a hot chocolate," Karen soothed, realising how upset her friend was.

"I'm so sorry. It's just that it isn't the first note I've received," she admitted as they walked to the cafe.

Karen sat her friend in a window table and went to

get the drinks.

"There you are - one hot chocolate complete with cream and marshmallows. Guaranteed to make everything better." Karen placed two mugs on the table.

"Thank you."

"So how long has this been going on?"

"I had a note, pushed through my door a while back, complimenting me on the jumper I had worn the night before. I thought it was from Mick because I had been over to see him, but he knew nothing about it."

"It sounds like you have a secret admirer. It's not something to get upset about." Karen gently held her arm. "This person has never threatened you, have they?"

"No but it's awful not knowing who it is. Everywhere I go I feel like I'm being watched." Chloe twirled a strand of hair nervously round her forefinger.

"It doesn't sound like anything to worry about. He's probably someone really shy who doesn't know you already have a boyfriend."

"You're probably right," Chloe agreed, and drained her mug. "We'd better hurry now or we will miss the start of the film."

CHAPTER 18

Friday December 13th

Friday the thirteenth; Chloe was hoping that it wasn't a bad omen for the Christmas Carol service at the farm. The whole place had been carefully decorated and the nativity scene was all set for the school children at the end of the big barn, which usually held the tractor and the specially designed trailer that was used for visitor rides around the fields. Hot punch and a child friendly alternative would be served after the singing, along with mince pies, which she and Sally had been helping Dawn to bake yesterday.

The small brass band from Bulls Cross were first to arrive and set themselves up in one corner of the barn. The coach carrying the children from the local school followed soon after, and the teachers and assistants organised their pupils on the benches each side of the manger. It wasn't long before the parents and villagers were all assembled and Toffee the donkey was led in by James' son Christopher along with the two children who had been chosen to be Mary and Joseph for the evening. The band struck up the first notes of Little Donkey and the children sang, their breath visible in the cold night air.

After an initial couple of songs from the children, the WI performed a set before everyone else was invited to sing a few well-known carols from their printed sheet ending with a rousing chorus of Oh Come All Ye Faithful. There followed a chance for photos to be taken before drinks and mince pies were served. Christopher went round shaking a bucket for donations, which this year would be given to the local Air Ambulance.

With the last mince pie gone and folk gradually leaving, Chloe accepted a non-alcoholic punch offered to her by James and sat on a bale next a friend who had been playing in the band.

"A good turn out," Anne remarked, as she packed her cornet away in its box.

"Yes. I think everyone enjoyed it."

"I hope this is going to be an annual event; it's such a good way of getting into the Christmas spirit."

"It was fun organising it, and if James is willing, I can't see why it shouldn't be."

"Are you ready, Anne?" asked another band member.

"That's my lift home." Anne got up, brushing off the straw which had stuck to her black trousers, and left with a little wave. "Good to see you again, Chloe."

By now most people had left or were making their way to the door, so Chloe grabbed a black plastic sack and busied herself clearing up the paper plates and plastic glasses before heading off herself. It had been a long day and she was meeting Mick at the Bull later for a meal.

She stepped out into the crisp evening air and looked up to see Orion clearly shining in the dark blue star-lit sky. It was no surprise to find a frost had already formed on her car windows so it was a while before she was able to leave.

Feeling rather Christmassy she chose a festive red dress to wear with knee-high black boots before hurrying back out. It was eight-thirty when she drove into the car park at the pub.

Mick was standing at the bar talking to the landlord about darts when she entered the lounge and was obviously impressed by her choice of outfit. He gave her a bear hug and kissed the top of her head.

"Wow! You look amazing," he whispered before letting her go.

"Thank you."

"Mine host has tucked us away over here," he said as he led her to a corner table, on which there was a tea-light candle, a single red carnation in a shot glass and a printed menu at each place setting.

They made their choices and Mick returned to the bar to order.

"How did the Carol Concert go?" he asked as he sat down.

"Very well," she said, as she took a sip of her tonic water. "I'm hoping to convince James that it should be an annual event." She went on to tell him about an hilarious poem entitled "The Week Before Christmas" which a lady from the WI had written especially for the occasion.

"I'm so proud of you," Mick smiled as he held her hand. "I wish I could have been there."

"Maybe next time," she said. "Christopher was looking forward to counting the coins in his bucket. There was a really good crowd with some late comers having to stand at the back. If we do it again next year we will have to use the bigger barn."

As they chatted over their meal, Chloe thought it was like old times again; they seemed closer now than ever. The evening left her with a warm glow and she found herself singing happily on her drive home.

It was after eleven when she got there, so the heating had gone off and it was freezing cold in the flat. She boiled the kettle and filled a hot water bottle before heading to bed and had only just nodded off when she was startled by the ringing of the house phone in the living room.

"Who the hell can that be at this time of night?" she muttered as she padded anxiously across the landing.

"Hello?"

There was silence and then a click followed by music playing as a voice began to sing. She didn't recognise the song but caught the words 'beautiful in red' before the line went dead. She dialled 1471 but as before, the number was withheld. It sent a shiver down her spine to know that whoever it was had seen her tonight. In a panic, she ran down to double check that she'd locked the door, and peered through the little window, but couldn't see anyone loitering outside. It must have been someone in the crowded pub.

She climbed back into bed but she couldn't get the phone call out of her head and she lay wide awake for hours. When she finally drifted off to sleep she was disturbed by dreams about a faceless predator chasing her across the fields of the farm where she worked.

CHAPTER 19

Friday December 20th

Paula closed the door to her room and dragged her wheelie suitcase out to the street. Term was finished and she was off back home for the holidays. It was a while since her last trip, and she had made a friend on the course so hadn't been feeling so lonely.

While she waited for her train, she thought about the handsome guy in the suit and wondered if he would be travelling today. In her reverie he spoke to her and she found out more about him. Her daydream was abruptly interrupted by the arrival of the First Western, and she was surprised to realise that there were now a lot more folk waiting on the platform since she had arrived.

It wasn't easy to find a seat near the luggage rack so I had to stand near the sliding door. I had to make sure my case was safe because it took ages last weekend to find those presents. There was a hold up at Bristol Parkway and I was worried that I would miss my connection but luckily that one was late too so I'm here now enjoying the comforts of home.

I managed to get a double seat at Cheltenham when a couple got off but sadly the handsome hunk wasn't travelling today.

CHAPTER 20

Friday December 20th

After last week's concert the farm was closed to visitors until February when the first of the lambs were due to be born. The first job today was to write letters to the school and WI to thank them for their contributions to the event and inform them of the magnificent sum of £238 that had been raised for the Air Ambulance. Chloe was then able to concentrate on adding news and photos to the website. Conversion of an old outbuilding had now begun and a few smart lodges had already been added to the campsite.

The smell of beef casserole met her as she opened the door that evening. Mick was coming round for dinner later and she had put the ingredients into the slow cooker this morning. She picked up the mail from her doormat and leafed through the envelopes as she climbed the stairs trying to guess who the Christmas cards were from by the handwriting on the envelopes. She tossed them onto the coffee table, kicked off her shoes and put the kettle on for a drink, which she carried through to the living room to sit and open her mail.

One by one she opened the envelopes and six of her guesses had been correct. She studied the next one where the name and address was printed which made it difficult. As she opened the card, which had a chirpy looking robin on the front, something fell out onto the floor. She bent down to pick it up and found it was a photo of her singing merrily at last week's carol concert. She smiled then looked to see who had sent it but they had forgotten to sign the card. The last envelope contained a not so welcome bill so she put it to one side then rummaged in the unit drawer for her blue tack and made short work of sticking her cards on the living room door before propping the photo up against a candlestick on the shelf. She needed to make the dumplings to go into the casserole before changing into a sexy black dress. This was the first time that Mick had been to her flat since his accident and she wanted to make a good impression with a tried and tested meal.

Judging from the appreciative look on his face as she opened the door, her efforts weren't wasted.

"Something smells good," Mick smiled as he handed her a bottle of Merlot.

The casserole was cooked to perfection and Mick seemed suitably impressed. After their meal, they snuggled up on the sofa and watched a Christmas film before spending their first night together in a long time. The next morning Mick slipped quietly out of bed and surprised Chloe with a cup of tea.

"That's a nice photo of you on the shelf," he said. "Who took it?"

"I have no idea. Probably one of the parents from the local school as I stood next to the children during the carols. It came in a Christmas card but there was no signature."

"Well, it must be someone you know very well from what they've written on the back."

"I didn't look at the back - what does it say?"

"Take a look for yourself."

Chloe jumped out of bed, hurried through to the living room and snatched the photo from the shelf, knocking the china candlestick which crashed onto the floor as she did so. Flipping the picture over, she found the words, 'My beautiful Chloe.'

A wave of nausea came over her and she looked up to see Mick, who was standing in the doorway watching her, arms folded.

"Are you sure you don't know who it's from?" he asked.

"Positive. I haven't a clue."

Should she tell him about the other notes? Probably not, because he would wonder why she hadn't told him earlier.

"I really have no idea who it is from," she assured him. "You do believe me, don't you?"

He shrugged, obviously not convinced and paused before answering, "I know it's been hard for you, with me losing my memory and I would understand if you wanted to move on with someone new."

She wasn't expecting this. She walked up to him, held him at arm's length and looked into his eyes.

"Mick, I love you and only you. I really have no idea who sent that photo."

He stood staring at her and she could see he wanted to believe her but wasn't sure.

Desperate to change the subject, she asked, "Would you like some porridge? It'll help keep out the cold."

Mick nodded towards the open cupboard. "I'd prefer Cornflakes, if that's all right. I've got to leave soon. I said I'd meet Pete at eleven and I've got to go home and change first."

Chloe grabbed the packet and handed it to him. The atmosphere had turned decidedly frosty and although there was plenty of time, he left straight after his breakfast, giving her a quick peck on the cheek as he left.

Karen had suggested that she and Chloe go into town today. Chloe still had presents to buy for her family and she needed to get something special for Mick so had readily agreed. It was decided that they would meet by the statue outside the shopping centre.

Town was already heaving with shoppers as they struggled to find appropriate gifts. There were women with full carrier bags and men wandering aimlessly with glazed expressions on their faces and no idea what to buy. After a good two hours of browsing and queuing they decided to stop off at a small cafe for something to eat. While there Chloe told Karen about the photograph and the unsigned card.

"There's nothing I can do," she shrugged. "There is no actual threat, and going to the police would be a waste of my time and theirs. I just wish they would stop."

"It's a shame that you hadn't already told Mick about the other note."

"We've been getting on so well and I didn't want to bother him with such a trivial thing."

"Have you thought of who it might be?"

"I've been racking my brains and I can't think of anyone. It spooks me because whoever it is knows where I work and where I live."

"Do you think it could be someone who goes running on a Saturday morning?"

"I had thought of Jeremy - Mick once joked that he had a soft spot for me - but I don't think he's the sort to play games like this."

The cafe was noticeably quieter by the time the two girls left and after another hour trudging round Chloe finally found the ideal jumper for Mick, and with her list complete suggested a wander round the small Christmas market they had bypassed earlier. before catching the bus back to Karen's home.

Karen found a dainty glass ornament for her Christmas tree and although Chloe didn't buy anything she enjoyed looking at the wares and soaking up the atmosphere. It wasn't far from there to the bus station and a short wait for their double-decker to arrive.

They left the bus at the market square where the big decorated fir stood, as it always did, outside the town hall, and a group of people dressed in Victorian costume were getting ready to sing carols nearby. Their route took them along the High Street, where coloured lights were strung up between the lamp posts, then past houses where large twinkling reindeer, bells and icicles adorned the walls. They arrived at Karen and Pete's maisonette to find the boys in good spirits having already toasted their team's win with a few cans of lager.

CHAPTER 21

Tuesday December 31st

Christmas was over in a flash. Chloe had spent the week at her family home in the Cotswolds - a chance to relax, spend some time with her family and enjoy her mother's home cooking. Alex and her fiancé had joined them for a buffet tea on Boxing Day and she had been able to hit the sales with her sister yesterday.

She pulled into her drive after a rather irksome journey, with heavy rain between Tewkesbury and Worcester on the motorway. Welcomed home by the beacon of the security light as she dragged her suitcase, with some difficulty, over the gravel to her door, she ignored the pile of envelopes on the mat and heaved her luggage up the stairs. It took a while to unload the car and she picked up the mail on the final ascent, shoving it into a carrier bag full of presents to look at later.

After a quick freshen-up and a splash of perfume she galloped back downstairs and was soon driving towards Bulls Cross where she had arranged to meet Mick at the pub. It may have been good for them to have some time apart but she hoped that he had missed her as much as she had him.

The temperature had dropped and she could see her breath as she crossed the pub car park. She soon spotted Mick playing pool with one of the locals. He was wearing his new pullover and beamed when he saw her heading his way. He fished out a fiver from his pocket.

"What would you like to drink?"

"A diet coke please."

Mick paid the barman.

"Take a seat. I've just got to beat this old codger and I'll be with you," he said as he patted the old boy next to him on the back amicably.

Chloe took her drink to a seat near the glowing flames of an open fire and waited for the game to finish, which, true to his word, Mick easily won.

"It's so good to see you," he kissed her on the cheek. "Texting just isn't the same."

"I know. It's been nice spending time with the family but I have really missed you."

"I've got some good news. I went for a check-up this morning and the doc told me I can go back to work next week."

"That's fantastic!"

"It sure is. I have been going bonkers stuck at home

under Mum's feet. She suggested I get some invoices done but I haven't been able to as I still can't remember the jobs. The notes I'd made in my work diary haven't helped at all," he sighed.

"It's a really good start to the brand new year. I just wish you could regain those lost months."

"I know I still haven't remembered meeting you for the first time or the time we spent together before my accident, but when I looked at you from my hospital bed and found out that you were my girlfriend I thought how lucky I was."

Chloe blushed. "I was afraid I'd lost you, but I think we are just as good now as we were before."

They made their way to the lounge to enjoy the entertainment. The landlord's daughter, who was at home from Drama school, sang a medley of songs from the shows before a local duo took over for the rest of the evening. A large buffet had been arranged for the regulars and at midnight, as the church bells chimed the hour, everyone left the pub to watch as rockets zoomed up bursting high above them in colourful shapes against the dark blue starry sky. Mick hugged Chloe and kissed her.

"Happy New Year, darling."

Chloe had said her goodbyes and left alone. It was as much as she could do to keep her eyes open and all she needed was a good night's sleep. To prove it she didn't see the light of day until 9.30. Mick would be over later and she decided to have a lazy morning, starting with a leisurely breakfast of toast and marmalade.

Later while she was unpacking her carrier bags of sales shopping and presents she found the envelopes she had stowed away last night. They were mainly Christmas cards that had been pushed through the door by friends and neighbours, and she smiled at a comment made on one from one of the badminton group. Her good humour drained away when she read the slip of paper in the next envelope. The hairs on the back of her neck bristled a warning.

"Missing you. I look for you every day, but you are not there."

She looked at the envelope - it had no address, just her name written there. She was going to have to tell Mick this time. He needed to know, and maybe he could help work out what deluded person was hounding her. It really scared her to think that she was being watched.

CHAPTER 22

Wednesday January 8th

Diane was sitting in Brenda's living room with a cup of tea, telling her all about the hectic Christmas she had enjoyed with the whole family at her house for dinner.

"I've probably put on a stone in weight with all the biscuits and chocolates I was given," she said with a contented sigh. "Anyway, that's enough about me. How did you and Robin enjoy your sunny getaway?"

"Oh, it was lovely! Funchal was so beautiful with everything lit up. The houses, bridges and streets were all decorated with bright coloured lights as well as the trees - even the palms near the harbour. There weren't any Christmas trees like we have but they had decorated conical artificial ones in prominent places.

"We relaxed by the pool quite a lot as the hotel was at the top of a very steep hill and, although it was nice to walk down into the city, it was a hard climb back up again. We signed up to go in a jeep to the start of a stroll along a levada, an irrigation channel, specific to Madeira, which they use to transport the water to the crops. It's a perfect way of getting right into the countryside and be at one with nature. We had the most amazing views of the valley deep below us. The jeep was waiting for us at the end to whisk us back to base. We had a couple of trips out too, including a ride on a wickerwork sledge down a steep village street."

"That sounds scary! So what was it like to be in a foreign land at Christmas? What was the meal like? Didn't it seem strange?"

"Well, it was odd not having a proper English Christmas dinner but they tried, bless them, and the food was very nice. We had Bolo Rei, or King's Cake, in the shape of a crown and decorated with dried fruit. "

"Well, it's good to share in their traditions, too, otherwise there's no point travelling all that way. Would you go away at Christmas again?"

"Probably not." Brenda's smile slipped a little. "I enjoyed the sunshine, and the temperature was a steady eighteen degrees, but it was a bit lonely after dinner. Robin would go to his room to read and there was no entertainment at the hotel, so I went back to my room and tried to find something on the TV; but there wasn't much other that the BBC news in English. I did find a couple of American films which they had subtitled in Portuguese."

"Do you have any photos?" Di asked, thinking it wise

to drop the subject.

"I picked them up this morning from the chemist and haven't had a chance to look at them yet." Brenda nipped to the kitchen and came back with a paper bag containing a photo wallet which she put to one side while she handed Diane a bottle of Madeira wine. "I bought this for you - I think you'll like it."

"Oh, Brenda, that is so kind of you. I'm sure I will." Diane took it and looked at the label before placing it on the floor by her handbag.

The ladies looked through the pictures together and Diane agreed that the Christmas lights in the city had been splendid. Brenda handed her a snap of Robin, taken on their walk with incredible views in the background. Not having seen him for some years, she was surprised to discover what a good-looking man he had become.

"With looks like his, he should have the girls flocking after him."

"The only girls he mixes with are other teachers - all a lot older than him and married."

"Our Sarah would be the right age and young Jade could do with a father," Diane suggested with a chuckle.

"I think he's happy as he is for now. I enjoyed that bingo night we had," Brenda added, quickly moving on.

"I like a game too - perhaps we should go more often. I've heard that the football club is thinking of starting a weekly session on a Wednesday night. I'll see what I can find out."

"Wednesday night is good for me because there isn't

usually a lot to watch on TV mid-week."

"I'll ask Mrs Young when I pick Jade up from school. Her other half plays for the firsts. I'll let you know," Diane said, casting a wary glance out at the gathering clouds. "That sky looks like rain and I put some washing out before I left; I'd better get home and rescue it."

CHAPTER 23

Friday January 17th

It was Chloe's 30th birthday and she had been spoilt at work, where she had shared an exquisitely decorated birthday cake made by Dawn. Her bosses had given her a framed picture by a local artist depicting sheep on a hillside meadow. There was also a huge basket of flowers from her colleagues along with a large box of chocolates from Chloe's favourite shop. As she struggled out of her car she was surprised to see Bob standing in his doorway.

"What lovely flowers," he exclaimed, as he came to meet her. "You look as if you could do with a hand."

"Hello, stranger. Thank you, I think I could."

"I'm over for a friend's birthday and thought I'd pop in to make sure the flat was okay - no leaks or such. Looks like it must be your birthday too."

"Yes, thirty today," she told him as he took the flowers from her and walked with her to her door.

There were cards on the mat, and he picked them up for her and followed her up the stairs.

"Thank you," she said, as he placed the basket on the landing table. "Would you like a drink, as it's a special occasion? I have some Prosecco in the fridge."

"That would be very nice," he smiled, and followed her into the kitchen.

She handed him the bottle to open while she reached into the cupboard for some glasses.

"Happy birthday," he said as they clinked flutes.

"Thank you," she smiled. "How's the flat coming on?"

"Very well - the decorating is all done and I can now start to get some furniture organised. You'll have to come and take a look some time."

"It's bound to be very different. Mrs Bridges was a bit old fashioned in her taste."

She noticed for the first time what an unusually bright shade of blue his eyes were and felt her face redden when he caught her staring at him. The conversation dried up, and Bob looked a bit awkward as he quickly drained his glass.

"Well, enjoy the rest of your day," he said, as he backed out of the room.

How embarrassing, she thought, hearing him dash off down the stairs.

She picked up the envelopes from the kitchen table and wandered into the living room. Passing the flowers she decided they looked just right where they were on the landing table. There was a card from her parents with a Next gift voucher, and a small parcel from her sister containing a picture frame, hand decorated with a mosaic of coloured mirror tiles in various shades of pink which would match her bedroom. It housed a photo of her with Alex when they were a lot younger, playing on the beach at Weymouth. She was still smiling when she opened the next card which depicted a large vase of flowers. Inside was written, "I will buy you flowers every day when you are mine."

She sat down heavily in her armchair. "Not today. Not on my birthday. Why won't he just leave me alone?"

Angry and upset, she tore the card up. She took the scraps to the kitchen and dropped them into an empty tuna can on the draining board, rummaged in the drawer for some matches and watched as the fragments of card turned to ash.

Mick had said he would pick her up at seven thirty and she would have to hurry now if she was going to be ready. She chose a dress in several shades of green.

Bang on seven thirty Mick was at the door dressed smartly in a navy suit with pale blue shirt and royal blue silk tie. Chloe put on her warm woollen coat and hand in hand they walked to where their taxi was waiting. Mick gallantly opened the door for her before sliding in beside her. "Happy birthday, sweetheart," he said, his eyes warm.

At the restaurant they were greeted by a waiter in black suit and bow tie and shown to a candle-lit table in a cosy nook. The waiter held out her chair and as she sat she found there was a small wrapped package on her placemat. She opened it to find a silver pendant in the shape of a flower with five garnets set around what looked like a pearl.

"The man in the shop told me that garnet was your birthstone," Mick said, getting up to fasten it round her neck.

"It's beautiful," she told him and gave him a hug.

"I have another surprise for you." He beamed as he sat down. "I remember the first time I met you at that party. You walked in and I couldn't take my eyes off you. I was so happy when I plucked up the courage to speak to you and you told me that you had noticed me too."

"Your memory's back?" Chloe was so moved she felt tears prickling at her eyes. "That's made my day!"

Over a delicious meal accompanied by a bottle of Italian wine, Mick told her about the other things he had remembered. One thing was still locked away though, and that was the night when he had been mown down so near to home.

After their meal they walked the short distance to Pete and Karen's local where their friends were waiting for them in the lounge. Karen handed over a parcel which contained a set of four wine glasses, etched with a delicate grapevine design. Pete passed her a bag containing a bottle of Chardonnay. There was already Asti in an ice bucket on the table and he poured them each a glass.

"A toast to the birthday girl," he said.

"The birthday girl!" the others joined in.

A shop-bought birthday cake arrived, dutifully covered in thirty candles. Chloe laughed as the barmaid asked her to blow them out quickly as last week a similar amount of candles had set the fire alarm off.

She managed to extinguish the flames in two goes as the whole lounge was encouraged to join in with a raucous rendition of Happy Birthday, much to her embarrassment.

The cake was whisked away again and slices returned on plates with the rest boxed up for Chloe to take home with her. As they ate Mick told the others about how his memory had returned. Hearing this Pete poured the rest of the sparkling wine.

"This is really a night for celebrations," he exclaimed.

"So when did you start to remember?" Pete asked.

"It was about a week ago. Chloe was wearing the same dress that she had on the first time I saw her. I didn't say anything at the time, just in case, and I wanted to surprise her on her birthday."

"I don't know how you've managed to keep it secret."

"It's been difficult, I can tell you."

"I can't begin to tell you how happy this has made me," Chloe beamed.

CHAPTER 24

Saturday January 25th

After a cold but enjoyable 5K in the morning sunshine, Chloe had been chatting to a new girl and was now running late. She rushed past the open door of the downstairs flat and was surprised to hear music coming from inside. She recognised the unmistakable voice of Sting but couldn't recall the name of the song. She was humming it as she reached the top of the stairs, although she still had no idea of the words. This was going to bug her now until she remembered.

    Karen arrived half an hour later, which hadn't given her chance to wash up the breakfast things, but she knew her friend wouldn't judge her. They were going to spend a girlie day doing each other's nails, and watching a romantic chick flick, and it wouldn't hurt to have a small glass of fizz before they headed into town to meet up with the boys later.

"I'll just sort the dishes, and then I need your help to find something," Chloe said as they plodded up the stairs.

"What have you lost?"

"My new garnet pendant, which Mick gave me for my birthday. I was going to wear it last night but I couldn't find it. I'm sure it's in the bedroom somewhere. I remember Mick taking it off for me because I was worried it would become tangled in my hair during the night. I was sure I had put it back into its box and slipped it into the top drawer of my dressing table, but it's not there.

"It can't have gone far. I'm sure we'll soon find it."

"I hope so." Chloe squeezed washing up liquid into the bowl.

They systematically went through every drawer in the bedroom, moved furniture and even looked in the wastepaper basket, but there was no sign of the missing necklace.

"I think I'm losing my marbles. It's not the only thing that's gone missing." Chloe sat on the edge of the bed. "I bought a lovely warm mustard-coloured jumper for work and couldn't find it when I wanted to wear it.

"It'll turn up when you least expect it," Karen said.

Chloe looked thoughtful. "I suppose Mick may have put the pendant in his pocket without thinking," she mused. "But how can I ask him without admitting that I've lost it?"

"Are you sure you haven't worn it since - to work

maybe?"

"I'm positive. It's not the sort of thing I would wear with a jumper and I hadn't been anywhere to dress up since my birthday."

"Well, we know it's not here, anyway. Where shall I set up my things?" Karen asked, looking around for an electric socket.

"The kitchen table would be best. We'll have a coffee before we make a start."

They chattered as they both chose their preferred colour to paint their nails. Chloe picked out a pretty dark green, saying it might be a good match for her bridesmaid's dress so it wouldn't hurt to see what it looked like on. As she brushed on the first layer Karen asked her if she had heard from her secret admirer recently.

"Just an unsigned birthday card last week saying I would get flowers every day from him. I tore it up and burnt it. It only dawned on me later, but how did he know it was my birthday?"

"It must be someone you know. It wouldn't be anyone on social media, would it?"

"Nah - my friends are mainly girls and relations plus a few work colleagues. I can't imagine it would be one of them."

CHAPTER 25

Friday February 14th

The sun had risen in a spectacular array of reds and pinks this morning. Large drifts of snowdrops adorned the verges on Chloe's drive to work. Spring wasn't far away now.

The workforce were all getting ready for the opening of the new farm shop at the beginning of March and everyone had been roped in to help. Geoff and James fitted some of the shelving yesterday, and first thing this morning they had taken a delivery from In a Jam, a local preserve maker. Chloe's task for today was to price up the jars of marmalade, jams and pickles and to arrange them on the shelves. James and Dawn wanted everything they stocked to be sourced from within a five mile radius. The meat, eggs and milk came from the farm itself, and Dawn was taking a course on how to make cheese and yoghurt. Ladies from the WI were making cakes and biscuits, and they would get their bread from a nearby artisan bakery.

A van drove into the yard; Chloe noticed it was from Floresta, a rather up-market florist, and being nearest she opened the door to him.

"Flowers for Sally Jones," he announced loudly.

Sally heard and came rushing over. The delivery man handed her a pink hessian-covered box containing an array of carnations and roses of a similar hue accompanied by white alstroemeria tinged with delicate pink markings.

"They're beautiful," Chloe told her. "Does it say who they're from?"

Sally looked at the valentine card which came with the flowers. "Of course it does. My Alan wouldn't want anyone else to get the benefit," she laughed.

Chloe had dropped a hint to Mick about how romantic it was to receive flowers and secretly wished that they had been for her.

She carried on emptying all the cartons and re-arranging the goods until she was happy with her display. The postman had been and there were a couple of bookings for school visits after Easter, so she wandered to her little office and set about logging them onto the computer before putting together information packs for the teachers, outlining what would be happening on the farm during their visit.

She was about to head back to the shop when the door opened and James came in backwards clutching a bouquet of a dozen red roses and placed them on Chloe's desk. "That boyfriend of yours seems to have come up trumps," he chuckled as he left the room.

Chloe opened the little card to find the florist had written, "To my beautiful Chloe." She was on cloud nine for the remainder of the afternoon and kept looking at the blood red flowers where they stood on top of the filing cabinet in a metal bucket she had found in one of the outbuildings. She was pleased she had sent Mick a card and tonight she would give him the large chocolate heart she had bought him, which should satisfy his sweet tooth.

She planned to have a long scented bath before getting ready to go out. She was looking forward to going to a much publicised concert in the city this evening and had been allowed to leave work early. Mick had managed to secure tickets as soon as the gig was announced, knowing how much Chloe would like to see The Rocking Bears. Originally a local group, they were now regulars in the charts. On arriving home the first thing she needed to do was find a vase and managed to unearth a large green glass beauty from the back of the cupboard under the sink. She arranged the blooms as best she could and set them prominently on display in the living room, took a photo and posted it on Facebook along with the caption "Feeling Loved".

When the doorbell sounded, she found Mick with one arm behind his back and a big grin on his face. Hugging her with the other arm he kissed her before handing her a small bunch of yellow freesias.

"You hinted that you would like some flowers, so being the ever-romantic boyfriend that I am, I bought you these," he smiled as he presented them to her.

Chloe felt sick as she looked at the flowers and went as white as a sheet.

"Whatever's wrong?" he asked as she turned and ran upstairs.

"I had a delivery at work today," she cried as he followed her.

Mick saw the roses, strode across the room and grabbed them from the vase. He threw them against the wall, showering water over the coffee table. Chloe had never seen him so angry.

"They must have been from your other man. Your secret admirer," he snarled, his romantic gesture now well and truly overshadowed.

"I thought they were from you," Chloe sobbed.

Mick slumped into the nearest chair, still clutching his posy.

Chloe knelt on the floor in front of him and gently took the sweet smelling flowers from his hand. "These are worth so much more, because I know they are from you," she whispered as she looked deep into his eyes. "I love them, I really do."

She took them to the kitchen, where she found a special intricate white porcelain jug which her grandma had left her. She topped it up with water and filled it with the cheerful yellow flowers before placing it on the coffee table.

"I'm sorry," Mick indicated the red blooms strewn

over the floor.

"I don't want them." She put her arms around his neck. "But I do want you."

She kissed him, picked up the stems from the floor and walked purposefully through to the kitchen where she dumped them into the swing bin.

"The girl in the shop told me that freesias stood for thoughtfulness and trust. You are such a thoughtful person and I do trust you, I really do," Mick said, brightening a little.

Chloe's heart swelled as she realised just how much thought had been put into her present. She fetched the chocolate heart and gave it to him and was so happy to see him smile when he read the message that she had asked the chocolate shop to ice onto it.

CHAPTER 26

Monday February 17th

Diane was ready and waiting when the dark green Ford Focus with her friend Brenda in the passenger seat pulled up outside her terraced house. It took a while for her to fasten her seat belt, but with Robin's help she was finally secured and they set off to the city.

She thanked him for offering to take them shopping.

"No problem. I want to have a look round the museum, with the idea of taking my class there in the summer term. Their topic is going to be Anglo Saxons and there are some wonderful artefacts there."

Robin turned the radio on so that he could hear any traffic reports, which made conversation rather difficult, as Diane couldn't hear what was being said in the front. Instead she watched what views there were from the motorway as they sped along. Just over an hour later, when they reached the city centre, Robin found somewhere to pull in.

"Take as long as you need and give me a ring when you are ready to go home, Mum."

It had started to rain and the ladies made a beeline for the shops in the Bullring.

"Apparently there is something called the Staffordshire Hoard at the museum which he wants to see, then he thought he might go down to the canal and have a walk, so I do hope this rain will have stopped or it won't be very pleasant." Brenda said as they entered the shopping centre.

First stop was a big department store, with a whole floor dedicated to ladies' fashion. Brenda soon found a fitted navy blue dress with a design of red and white rosebuds which would go very well with a red jacket she already had. Diane was finding it more difficult. She had been told that she was not to buy anything in any shade of green, which was fine by her as she had her heart set on finding something in peach - a colour which didn't appear to be in vogue this year.

After a snack for lunch, the ladies left the bustle of the Bullring and were pleased to find the ground had dried up from earlier and the sun was trying to burn through the cloud. They pressed on to the nearby streets and it was in the window of a small, independent boutique that Diane found the dress of her dreams. It was a raspberry pink lace overlay dress, and Brenda smiled when she saw how well it looked on her friend. The assistant found a bolero jacket to go with it and tried to persuade Diane that she needed a hat, a suggestion which was quickly and politely dismissed.

It was after four o'clock when they finally left the shop, Diane already thinking that if she could lose a few pounds by the big day the dress would look even better. Brenda phoned her son, who said that he had walked further than he had intended and it might take some time to get to them. He suggested a cafe near to them, where they could go and have a drink while they waited for him. They readily agreed. Now that they had achieved their goals, they both realised that their feet were killing them.

The ladies were sated but tired when Robin collected them and Diane was very soon snoring loudly in the back seat while he chatted enthusiastically to his mother about the exquisite items that had been unearthed a decade ago from where they had lain since the 7th century. Pieces of weapons and crosses in gold and silver in exceptionally good condition considering their age.

Di woke feeling disoriented as the car glided into her road, and stubbed her toe when she struggled to get out. She thanked Robin again for taking them and waved goodbye as the red glow of the tail lights vanished round the corner and out of sight. One more last effort, she thought, as she hobbled up the short garden path.

CHAPTER 27

Thursday February 20th

Chloe was missing Mick. She hadn't seen him since Sunday night as he was in bed with flu – the real thing, not 'man flu' - and was feeling pretty ropey by all accounts. Not wanting her to catch it, he had insisted that she shouldn't visit, but thanks to modern technology they had been able to keep in touch. Although he told her he was feeling a lot better, he had struggled to keep his eyes open last night when she spoke to him on Skype, so she had kept it short and retired early to the warmth of her duvet, and ended up watching television until the small hours. She had not been sleeping well. Coming home one night earlier in the week she had noticed a strange perfumed smell which she didn't recognise, and her bedside light had been on, when she had been sure she'd turned it off before she had left for work that morning. Silly little things, but with the stalker preying on her mind more and more her imagination was running wild. Her home no longer felt safe, which was stupid. She needed to get a grip.

After a foggy start, it had been a dark and dismal wet day and Chloe was glad to be home. It had been a frustrating time at work with a dodgy internet signal and nothing going to plan. Now she was suffering with eyestrain and a thumping headache.

Fed up with her own company she decided that, although she was tired, she would still go to badminton tonight. The change of scene would do her good so she took a couple of paracetamol and prepared a cheese omelette which she ate at the kitchen table. Afterwards she put on a soothing CD to relax to as she caught up with the news on social media until it was time to leave.

With the headache now abating Chloe was looking forward to taking the annoyances of the day out on the court. It was still raining, and every now and then a big soft flake of snow settled amongst the raindrops on her windscreen and quickly melted before the wipers swished it away. She hoped it wouldn't come to much more before she left for home.

As she slammed the shuttlecock over the net she was glad she had come, and later enjoyed a hot chocolate with her partner after thrashing the opposition.

It was snowing gently as she eased her way out of the tight parking spot in the leisure centre car park, and she was glad that she didn't have to drive far as there was already a light covering on the untreated country lanes. Mesmerised by the large white feather-like shapes which were now flying towards her windscreen she opened the window a crack to allow the cold air to hit her face and prevent her from nodding off. She drove slowly and was relieved when she finally pulled into the drive.

As she locked the car, she noticed footprints leading to and from her front door. They had been partially covered by freshly falling flakes, but there were indents where someone had walked.

She followed the tracks to her door, wondering who could have called. *I hope there isn't another anonymous note waiting for me,* she thought.

Holding her breath as she opened the door, she felt for the light switch and heaved a sigh of relief as she found nothing on the doormat although there was a small puddle on the lino still from when she had come home earlier. On reaching the landing she clicked on every light before gingerly peering into each room and was relieved to find herself alone. Tired from her exertions, and because the heating had already gone off, she made her way straight to bed.

She had a fitful night, waking with a start, only an hour after she had fallen asleep. In her dream she was being chased through a snowy landscape by someone unknown and had woken as their footsteps were almost upon her. Wide awake now, she could feel the beating of her heart in her chest and sleep was impossible. After tossing and turning for a while she spent some time playing silly games on the iPad to try and dull her wakeful brain. She must have dozed off eventually as she woke to the shrill sound of her alarm at seven.

Although it wasn't far to drive to work, she was pleased to see the snow had nearly all gone with the return of the rain during the night.

It was definitely a day for porridge and she found some blueberries in the fridge to sprinkle on top. With that in one hand and a strong black coffee in the other she made her way to the living room where she could sit by the gas fire.

Her lovely freesias were lying on the coffee table next to their overturned jug. She must have knocked them over yesterday evening before she went out. Putting her breakfast aside, she went to refill the jug, and replaced the flowers, but she doubted they would survive. If only she had come in here last night, she may have been able to save them.

CHAPTER 28

Saturday February 29th

There was a cold north easterly wind whistling through the yew trees in the nearby churchyard. Karen rubbed her hands together as she stood shivering and waiting for Chloe to answer the door. When she finally appeared, Karen was surprised at how drained she looked.

"Chloe, you don't look at all well."

"I'm fine. I'm just feeling really jittery. Come in, and maybe you can tell me if I'm being stupid."

"Are you sure you've not got the flu, like Mick?"

"It isn't that – it's this." Chloe picked up an envelope from the table and handed it to her.

Karen opened the envelope and took out the slip of paper. She read out loud, "'I was so pleased to smell that you were wearing the perfume I sent you.' What perfume? Who gave it to you?"

"I don't know. I hardly ever wear scent but I was feeling a bit down when I got home from work on Wednesday. I was missing Mick, and it had been such a grey and dreary afternoon that before you and I went out that evening, I splashed on a sample I received in the post some time back."

"I remember thinking at the time that it was unusual for you to wear perfume I still don't understand though."

"I had assumed it was a sample because I'm always clicking on special offers and have had plenty of things turn up before, but it must have been from the weirdo that keeps messaging me. I'm scared now, because he must have been standing really close to me to have been able to smell the perfume."

"Oh, love, no wonder you feel jittery." Karen gave her a hug before looking at the postmark on the envelope. "Birmingham - that's not a great deal of use. Why don't they postmark things locally any more?"

The two girls had been to a pottery painting evening on Wednesday night. It was an event aimed at the ladies with a glass of Prosecco included in the price. They'd enjoyed a good laugh as they painted their mugs in various jolly colours, which would only become properly apparent once they had been fired. The session had finished a good forty five minutes before their bus was due to leave, so rather than hang around in the cold, they had popped into the warm haven of the nearby pub for a final drink.

"There weren't any men at the pottery, so he must have been in the pub," Chloe reasoned.

"Unless it's a woman," Karen said, trying to lighten the mood.

"Oh strewth, I never even gave that a thought." Chloe made her way to the living room window and peered out then started to pace. "Everywhere I go I wonder if that person is there watching me. It is really messing with my head. I've been having dreadful dreams where there is someone in my room but when I look properly it is only a shadow and I wake up in a cold sweat." Chloe slumped onto the sofa. "I'm scared, Karen, I really am. Every time I'm here on my own I wonder where he is and whether he knows I'm alone."

Karen knelt down beside her, and took her hands. "Try not to worry," she soothed. "You live on the first floor. No-one can get to the windows, and with the door locked you are safe."

Chloe forced a little smile. "Yes, I'm safe here," she said, more because Karen wanted to hear it than because she believed it.

Karen placed her hands on her friend's shoulders and looked into her eyes. "Come on, the spa is booked from one o'clock and I think you are in need of some serious pampering and relaxation."

Mick was now fully recovered, but Chloe had found him somewhat subdued since his arrival earlier. He seemed happy enough and she thought it was the after-effects of his illness, but later realised he was deep in thought.

"What's the matter?" She touched him, which made him jump.

He stared at her for a couple of seconds before asking, "What are the Ides of March?"

"That's a strange question. From what I remember it was something to do with the Romans and Julius Caesar," she replied. "Why do you ask?"

He got up and went to his coat, which was hung over the banister at the top of the stairs, and took something from the pocket.

"This was stuck underneath my windscreen wiper. I have no idea when it was put there because I haven't used the van all week." He handed her a soggy scrap of paper.

Chloe opened it carefully and read out loud, "Beware the Ides of March."

She reached for her laptop. "Come on. We'll have a look on here and see what it says." She typed the phrase into her search engine.

"Well, apparently it was a warning given to Julius Caesar and he was subsequently killed on that date."

"When is the Ides?"

"The fifteenth."

All the colour left Mick's face. "The last time I had a warning, I was knocked down soon afterwards. Do you think this is connected?"

"I didn't know about the warning at the time, but while you were in hospital a plain-clothed policeman came to see me, asking about any ex-boyfriends that might be jealous of you and wish to harm you. It may not be connected, but do you think it could have anything to do with the person who has been stalking me?"

"It's possible. It's not long until the fifteenth of March and I think we need to speak to the police."

"I still have that guy's card somewhere." Chloe emptied her handbag onto the coffee table and began looking through all the old receipts and store loyalty cards until she found what she was looking for.

"Here it is - DI Willis. It's got a mobile number."

She carefully punched the numbers into her phone and was pleased to get through quickly.

"Hello, this is Chloe Thornby. You came to see me a while ago when my boyfriend was involved in a hit and run."

An hour later DI Willis was sitting in the armchair in Chloe's living room.

"It may be nothing," Mick said as he passed the drying scrap of paper to the detective, "but after what happened the last time I had a warning, I have to say this has worried me."

"It could be someone's idea of a joke; but I think we need to take it seriously," Willis replied. "Can you think of anyone who would want to harm you?"

"No. I thought the message scrawled on my van was just kids having a laugh. I haven't had a cross word with anyone and the only customer who might have got the wrong idea was a local businessman whose wife was a bit flirty and kept asking me to change this and that from the original specification."

"Who is this businessman?"

"Gerald Stevens. He works away a lot and I think his wife gets a bit bored, but nothing untoward happened and I don't seriously think he would have knocked me down. I still think it was an accident really and the driver either didn't know they'd hit me, or were too scared to stop."

"All the same, I would still like his address."

"It's in my book at home. I'll let you have it."

"Now, Miss Thornby, you say you have been getting gifts and letters from an unknown admirer?"

"Yes, although there has never been any threat. It's just unnerving as whoever it is knows where I live, where I work, places that I go to. I feel like I'm being stalked."

"When did this start?"

"Soon after Mick's accident. I had a note complimenting me on my jumper. No - I think the perfume arrived first, but I thought it was a free sample as there was no note with it. I'm pretty sure now that was from him as I received this letter this morning." She picked up the envelope from where she had put it earlier on the bookshelf and passed it to him. He took it carefully by the edges.

"Have you had a lot of these messages and gifts?"

"Flowers, cards, notes, strange phone calls where there is no one there when I answer."

"Do you have any of the other notes?"

"No. I threw them all away."

"I would like you to make a list of every one you can remember."

Willis then turned to Mick and held up the piece of paper he had given him. "I'll keep this, if you don't mind." He took a plastic bag from his jacket pocket and put the note and the envelope which Chloe had just given him into it.

"Yeah, sure."

"I've just thought of something." Chloe turned to Mick. "Can you remember the day you dropped me at the station to catch the train to Cheltenham?"

"We were a bit early and you were going to go and get a coffee."

"Yes. There was a guy there who was staring at me. I thought I recognised him but then realised I didn't. I thought it was a bit odd at the time but I'd forgotten it until just now."

"Can you remember what he looked like?" Willis asked.

Chloe closed her eyes to try to recall the scene.

"He had short dark hair and was average height. I'm sorry - that's all that I can remember."

"Have you noticed him anywhere since?"

"I don't think so."

"As soon as you can, bring that list to the police station in Forest-in-the-Green - and keep an eye out for anyone who seems out of place where you are. Possibly someone you know, who just happens to be there more than just on the odd occasion."

"What should I do - especially on the 15th of March?" Mick asked.

"Be vigilant."

CHAPTER 29

Sunday March 8th

Sauntering back from the village shop with his newspaper Mick almost bumped into Chloe's part-time neighbour, all togged up and ready to go for a run. Bob waved, but didn't stop.

"I just saw Bob jogging out through the gate," he chuckled. "He really has gone over the top. I reckon he's spent a fortune on the kit - he certainly looks the part."

"He can obviously afford it and is probably trying to get fit. I should imagine his job would involve a lot of sitting around at a computer screen."

"I need to get fit too. I put on weight when my leg was in plaster and I need to do something about it. Do you fancy going swimming this afternoon?" Mick asked as he buttered his toast. "I was given some free tickets for the Spa at the leisure centre in town. They were well pleased when I fixed their boiler so quickly last week and said I saved them a lot of money in lost revenue."

"That sounds like a good idea; I haven't been swimming for ages. I'll treat you to a carvery afterwards at the pub on the same complex."

"You know the way to my heart," he smiled as he held her hand across the table.

"Alex rang while you were out. She's bringing Giles' niece over next weekend. Karen's Mum has finished the bridesmaids' dresses and we're going over there for a fitting on Saturday afternoon. If you're around in the morning, I would love you to meet her."

"Yes, that would be great. The boys are at home so I won't have to leave too early."

Mick tackled the washing up while Chloe went to look for her swimming costume. She came back with a modest black number along with a jazzy holiday beach towel and started looking in the kitchen drawers for a carrier bag.

"I've just remembered, I noticed a wet patch where you usually park your van when I got back yesterday morning. I think you might have an oil leak."

"I hope not - the van's only three years old. I'll check the level before we leave."

It was late morning when they left and Mick needed to collect his swimming gear from home on the way. The oil level was fine, but they hadn't gone far when Mick complained that the steering didn't feel quite right.

"It could be a slow puncture," he said. "I don't think

Dad's going anywhere today so I'll ask if I can borrow the car."

He drove steadily, and checked all four tyres when they arrived but they looked fine. His father was happy for him to take the car and he would arrange for his mate at the garage to look at the van tomorrow morning.

"I feel really good after that. We ought to go more often," Mick said as they walked hand in hand towards the Happy Wanderer. "We shouldn't have any trouble getting a table at this time of day."

Mick had worked up quite an appetite and helped himself to all the vegetables and trimmings that were available and still managed apple pie and custard which was included in the price.

"I've got to build my strength up," he declared when she questioned where he found room for it all.

It wasn't until Chloe had paid the bill and they got up to leave that they noticed how quickly it had filled up. There was quite a queue forming in the foyer as customers waited for a table to become free. They emerged into heavy rain and they had to dash back to the car park, trying to miss the puddles.

"Oh no – someone's scratched the door. They must have parked too close," Mick complained. "Why can't people be more careful? Dad's not going to be happy."

They were getting soaked, so they jumped inside as quickly as they could; the scratches would still be there later. The windows steamed up almost immediately and even with the heater fan on full it was difficult to clear them. They'd hardly left the car park when Mick's mobile rang out so Chloe took the call. It was Mick's dad. She put him on speaker phone.

"Mick, don't you ever check the fluid levels in your van?" he demanded.

"Yes, of course I do - regularly."

"Well, I had a look at it when you left, and there is next to no steering fluid in it. No wonder the steering wasn't responsive."

"There was plenty when I last checked it. It must have sprung a leak."

"It's a good job you didn't drive it far. You would have done a lot of expensive damage if it had gone completely dry."

Mick whistled through his teeth. "Thanks for checking it, Dad. Have you asked Jim if he can have a look at it tomorrow?"

"Yes - but you need to get it there first thing."

"I'll do that. Thanks, Dad.."

Their clothes were sticking to them when they arrived at the flat where Chloe insisted that Mick put his on the radiator to dry so he suggested, with a cheeky grin, that they watch TV in bed.

It was after midnight when he left in warm, dry apparel. The rain had finally stopped, but the wind was getting stronger.

Chloe locked the door behind him and padded back to bed but try as she might she just couldn't get back to sleep. She tossed and turned and kept hearing strange noises leading her to imagine all sorts of things. She finally dropped off, but woke again in a cold sweat from the recurring nightmare where someone was in her room watching her. So realistic was her dream that she pulled the duvet up as far as she could and lay listening as the wind battered against the rattling window.

CHAPTER 30

Saturday March 14th

It had been another very windy night but Chloe had slept better with Mick by her side. Although it had calmed down a bit by morning, she struggled to enjoy her run and failed to get a good time today. Jeremy had appeared, hoping to engage her in conversation, but stood just that bit too close. She nearly fell over as she backed away to avoid him touching her arm, and she left him looking shocked when she dashed off muttering that she needed to get home as she had visitors coming.

Alex and Becky had already arrived when she got home, had introduced themselves and were enjoying a cup of tea with Mick.

"Sorry - I got held up," she apologised as she rushed in.

"I thought you wouldn't be long so I made you one,"

Mick said as he went to fetch her mug from the kitchen.

They all sat chatting together for a while until Mick left to go home to get changed for the match, and the girls then piled into Alex's Golf for the drive to Forest-in-the-Green. They would pick Karen up and all go to her mother's house.

The fitting went well and Chloe and Becky were both thrilled with their dresses, which only needed minor alterations. They were of a similar design except that whereas Chloe's had thin straps, Becky's had little puff sleeves. The gold brocade ribbon looked stunning, and Alex was reassured that her wedding day was going to be perfect.

Alex had a text reminding her of her appointment with the florist. She had made the arrangement a couple of months ago and with her head all over the place had forgotten. It wasn't until 4pm so she had time to get there if she left straight away. Karen offered to take Chloe home and stayed chatting for a while when they got there. She left late afternoon as the boys would be home fairly early today with the match only being at West Bromwich. Chloe locked the door behind her.

She then lugged her small cylinder vacuum cleaner up the stairs, wondering for the umpteenth time why she hadn't got one of those new lightweight cordless ones. After giving the carpet a once-over she swept and mopped the kitchen floor while her freezer meal rotated in the microwave.

She turned the television on and settled down in her

preferred velour armchair to eat. The news was as dire as ever so she reached for her mobile phone to catch up with all the gossip. Someone had set fire to a local children's playground last night and there was a photo of the charred remains. A tree had fallen across a main road and narrowly missed a bus full of passengers, who were shocked but otherwise unhurt. Linda Simmonds had posted that she was feeling lonely so she sent a little message to cheer her up; that was the first one she had sent although she often 'liked' Chloe's posts. It was an old friend's birthday so she sent her a funny photo of them together when they were teenagers along with a birthday greeting. The phone beeped and she realised it was almost out of charge, so she turned it off and plugged it in. She glanced at the carriage clock on the mantelpiece and, as was often the case, time had flown and she was sent into a panic as she hurriedly cleared away her plate and re-applied her make-up. She and Mick had decided not to go anywhere tonight and would stay in, snuggle up together on the sofa with a drink or two and some snacks. There was a new thriller on TV at nine and they could find something to do until then.

Ready, she picked up a magazine to read while she waited for Mick. The doorbell rang and she galloped down to let him in. It wasn't Mick but Bob who was standing there.

"The postman tried to deliver this earlier," he held up a small parcel, "and asked if I would take it in for you."

"Oh, thank you, Bob. I wonder what it is. I can't

remember ordering anything," she told him as he entered his own front door.

She re-locked the door and scrutinised the package to see if there was a company name on the pre-paid label. There was nothing to indicate who had sent it. She nervously opened it and found an emerald green glass-bead necklace. "I know who this is from," she smiled. Alex had mentioned jewellery last week on the phone and she must have ordered it to come straight to Chloe. It was a shame it hadn't arrived earlier or she could have taken it to the fitting with her. She'd text her later to thank her.

Chloe picked up her magazine and returned to the article she had been reading. When she had finished it she threw it down on the coffee table. Where was Mick? He should be here by now. She turned on her phone in case there was a message from him. There wasn't. It was already eight-thirty and he was usually here by eight even when he had nipped in the pub for a quick celebratory pint. As the minutes ticked by, her initial anger was turning to anxiety and at nine o'clock she checked her phone again and sent a text: "Where are you?" She walked through to the living room and looked out of the window and tried to see if any vehicles were heading down the lane, then paced around the flat, getting more frantic by the minute and constantly going back to the window to stare out into the dark. Finally a text came through: "Where are you?" She clumsily hit the keys, typing, "At home." A few seconds later came the reply, "I'm on my way." No explanation. What was going on?

It was ten-thirty when Mick's van pulled onto the gravel drive. He got out and ran to the door.

"Where the hell of you been?" Chloe greeted him in the doorway.

"Looking for you," he replied.

"What do you mean, looking for me? I've been here all evening waiting for you." She turned and stomped up the stairs, closely followed by Mick trying to explain.

"I had a text earlier, telling me that you had been in an accident and that an ambulance had taken you to hospital. I rang the number to find out which hospital but there was no answer. I rang the police and they said there hadn't been any road traffic accidents that they knew of and that perhaps you had fallen or something like that. I tried your phone but there was no answer."

Chloe felt guilty now. He was always telling her she didn't need to turn her phone off when she charged it. "I'm sorry. I was charging it and it was turned off."

"I'm just pleased to see you fit and well." He took her in his arms and held her tight.

"We'll report this to DI Willis tomorrow morning. It's got to be connected to everything else that has been happening lately," Chloe said.

"I think you're right. I have the phone number it came from so they should be able to trace it," Mick reasoned. "Perhaps they'll be able to put a stop to it."

The wind was howling around the building and Chloe

didn't want Mick to leave again so soon but, ever mindful that the next day was the ominous Ides of March, he was determined to go home and stay put for the whole of Sunday. She kissed him goodbye and made him promise that he would ring her when he got there.

After he had phoned as promised, she made herself a hot chocolate lacing it with a good slug of rum to help her sleep and took it through to drink in bed while she read a chapter or two of her new book.

The wind seemed to have died down a bit and she was able to drift off to sleep quite quickly but woke at about one in the morning to strange noises which seemed, in her agitated state, to be in the flat. Too scared to leave her room she lay rigid with every muscle taut as she strained to hear if the noise started again. It must have been an hour before she was able to relax fully again, but by now she was wide awake and sleep eluded her. She heard the church clock strike three and decided she might as well try reading again as there was no way she would be able to sleep now.

The inauspicious date had arrived, and as the light from the rising sun crept through her unlined curtains, Chloe finally fell asleep.

CHAPTER 31

Sunday March 15th

After a night of tossing and turning Chloe would have liked a lie in this morning but she was too wound up. There wasn't much to look forward to today. Mick was intending to spend the whole day at home and she might as well give the flat a good tidy. Although on the surface it all looked fine, she had a habit of throwing things into the drawers in the living room unit - out of sight, out of mind. She might as well have a go at those after breakfast and see what could be binned. She sent a text to Mick asking him what he was planning to do today, put on her dressing gown and headed for the kitchen.

A text came from Mick to tell her he was finally changing the bathroom taps much to his mother's relief. She would ring him later for a chat.

With the first drawer emptied out onto the living room floor, Chloe started to sort through the post and other detritus that had amassed. She was glad she found the letter from the garage reminding her that her MOT was due - she had forgotten and would make an appointment tomorrow. With bank statements and other important papers in one pile and a heap of receipts and empty envelopes in another she was getting on well when she heard a knock at the door. She wasn't expecting anyone and it spooked her. She would pretend she was out and they would go away. She sat like a statue, hardly daring to breath. The bell rang. Still she sat rigidly to the spot. After what seemed like an age she slowly rose to her feet and crept towards the window to peer out and try to see if there was anyone nearby. It was impossible to see the front doorstep without opening the window and leaning right out and she didn't want anyone who might still be standing there to see her. There were two or three people in the lane but nobody obvious. At least one of them looked dressed to be going to the morning service at the church.

She quietly went back to the task in hand, and after filing the paperwork, chucking the rubbish into the waste paper bin and re-locating other things she was pleased to have a tidy drawer to show for it.

Her legs ached from sitting cross-legged on the floor and she decided it was time to take a break. She'd phone her sister.

"Hi Alex - it's me."

"Hi there Chloe. To what do I owe this pleasure?"

"Just thought it would be nice to have a catch up. You okay to talk?"

"Yes. Giles is out washing the car and I wasn't planning on doing much."

"I was just tidying out a drawer and found the necklace you sent. It's beautiful and I think it will go perfectly with the dress."

"You've lost me. What necklace?"

"Sorry, I thought as it had green glass beads it was from you. I must have ordered it myself and forgotten." she tried to make light of it. *Yet another thing to let the detective know about.*

"You obviously spend too much time shopping online."

"Guilty as charged. How are the wedding plans going?"

Alex went on to tell her about the flowers and the menu for the reception and an hour passed before they realised. Chloe was smiling when she hung up but her smile didn't last long as she remembered the necklace. She stormed through to the bedroom to retrieve it from the little drawer in her bedside cabinet and tossed it into the large kitchen pedal bin. She then remembered she should have kept it to show the detective and took it out again and put it back into the envelope it had arrived in.

She was really feeling rattled now and needed to calm down before she spoke to Mick. Having found tidying out the first of the two drawers therapeutic, she decided to set to on the other. First she chose a soothing Snow Patrol CD to listen to and decided to take the drawer to the kitchen table to go through it. With a cup of tea and the dulcet sounds of Gary Lightbody she enjoyed re-reading her recent birthday cards before piling them up to go in the recycling bin. She found an origami swan which Mick had made for her and carefully put it in the "to keep" pile.

With another tidy drawer and feeling more at ease she decided to phone Mick to find out how he was getting on.

"Hello, lover," Mick answered, having seen who was calling.

"Hi there. How's your morning been?"

"I had a bit of trouble getting the old taps off but I've got the new ones up and working now and I have been helping dad put some shelves up in the garage. What about you?"

"I have cleared out the two drawers in the living room unit. Spoke to Alex and she is in full swing with the wedding arrangements. I put in a special request for sherry trifle."

Mick laughed, knowing it was her favourite dessert.

"Dad wanted to go to the Bull before lunch but I managed to get out of it by saying I'd rather try some of his home-made sloe gin. I didn't want to tell him I was too scared to go out."

"So what have you got planned for this afternoon?"

"I'm sure there will be something on Sky Sports to keep me amused. What about you?"

"I think I'll find a good film to watch. Close the curtains to block out the grey skies and hunker down with a large glass of vino and a big bag of popcorn."

CHAPTER 32

Monday March 16th

Mick looked tired when he arrived to collect Chloe and told her that he had been suffering with a bad head all afternoon. They decided to stay in instead of going bowling and ended up watching an interesting documentary about the painted lady butterfly and its long journey to Britain. The camerawork was amazing, but before the programme was over Mick was having trouble with his vision and told her that he thought his headache was turning into a migraine.

"I haven't had one for years," he told her. "I need to lie down and sleep it off."

Chloe had read somewhere that migraine could often be brought on by stress and knew how worked up he had become over the last few days, and how scared of what could happen if he went anywhere yesterday. He went to crawl into bed, and she left him to get some sleep.

With Mother's Day fast approaching, Chloe leafed through a catalogue trying to find a gift for her mum but couldn't find anything suitable. Uninspired, she put it back in the cupboard and was about to go channel hopping with the remote when her mobile pinged. It was a message from Karen, asking if she wanted to go to the garden centre on Saturday afternoon as she intended to get a plant for her mother. The place she had suggested had so many other things as well as plants, so Chloe quickly started typing a reply with both thumbs, and was just finishing when the house phone started to ring. She pressed Send and dashed to answer it before it woke Mick who, when she had checked on him, had been sleeping peacefully .

"Hello."

Click. The other person had hung up. She immediately rang 1471 but the caller had withheld their number. She huffed and rammed the phone back on its base. This was happening too often. Normally it would have just been annoying, but that cop had seemed to think it was significant. A cold shiver enveloped her as she sat back down and stared at the handset. She wondered if there was any way she could block these calls.

With nothing on the television she decided she might as well go to bed and quietly climbed in beside Mick. Sleep evaded her as she listened to her boyfriend's breathing and her brain refused to allow her to rest. The church clock struck one and still Chloe was wide awake. She got up and padded into the living room, taking her book with her. She looked out to see what the weather was like and saw a car parked opposite the churchyard. There were no houses on that side of the road, so it was a strange place to park. It was too dark to see if anyone was inside it or not.

Startled by a noise behind her she spun round to find Mick with his parka jacket on.

"I need to go home. I have to pick up some parts from the merchant as soon as they open in the morning," he explained.

"Are you sure you're okay to drive?"

"Yes. I'm fine now. I'll text when I get home."

Reassured, Chloe accompanied him to the bottom of the stairs and kissed him goodbye. She locked the door behind him before returning to the window to watch him drive off and noticed that the car which she had seen only a few minutes earlier had already gone.

Chloe's feet had grown cold so she made her way back to the warmth of her duvet and eventually nodded off but was woken what seemed like minutes later by a dreadful scream. Her heart thumped as she listened, too scared to move a muscle and hardly daring to breathe. It was only when the hoarse yell came again that she realised what it was that had woken her; a vixen, looking for a mate. Knowing what it was didn't help, though, and yet again sleep became a distant memory.

Seven o'clock and the shrill, unwanted sound of her alarm signified morning. Tired and feeling totally drained, Chloe dragged herself out of bed. She thought about calling in sick but didn't want to spend the day alone in the flat. A hot shower should help to wake her up, but it took that and a strong black coffee with her slice of toast before she was anything like herself.

Last night's migraine had shown her that things were getting to Mick too. She hoped that the police would be able to track the owner of the mobile used to message him, then perhaps they could arrest whoever it was, and the two of them could resume their lives.

She sent a text to Mick to ask how he was feeling, and he quickly replied that he was fine. With her jacket buttoned up she picked up her car keys and left for work. As she locked the door she noticed that the tiny violets her mum had given her last year were beginning to bloom in the little border near her front door. She smiled to see them and bent down to take a closer look. There was something shining amongst the leaves. It was her pendant - but the chain had been broken into three pieces. She carefully picked it up and took it to her bedroom, where she placed it in her jewellery box. Glad as she was to have it back, even though she would need to buy a new chain, there were so many questions buzzing round her head. How it had got there, who had broken it – and why?

CHAPTER 33

Friday March 20th

Dawn had been busy in the kitchen this morning making scones for the sold-out Afternoon Tea being held in the village hall on Sunday. She brought one, smothered in strawberry jam, into the office for Chloe to enjoy with her afternoon cuppa.

Chloe thanked her as she placed it on the desk but Dawn lingered and eventually asked if Chloe was all right.

"Yes, I'm fine," she answered as she popped a tea bag into her mug.

"You've looked so tired recently," the older woman said. "You just haven't seemed yourself."

"I haven't been sleeping too well of late."

Dawn didn't reply but looked at her, hoping for a better explanation.

"I'm fine – really," Chloe repeated and gave her a weak smile, before picking up the scone. Dawn took this as her cue to leave.

I'm not fine though, Chloe admitted as she fumbled in her drawer for her packet of paracetamol.

She was finding it hard to concentrate and more than once found herself staring through the office window. It was as she was watching James herd the dairy cattle across from the fields to the milking parlour that she was shaken out of her daydream to the sound of a text on her phone. It was from Mick.

"I'm sorry but I can't make it tonight. Is it okay to ring you in a couple of minutes?"

She typed back, "Yes. I'm on my own in the office." She waited, drumming her fingers on the desk.

A few seconds later her mobile rang. She snatched it up.

"Hello."

"I thought it would be easier to talk than text. I got an email from someone the other side of Nottingham offering me good money for a couple of weeks' work. I need to go and meet him early tomorrow morning to assess the job, so I've arranged to stay with my aunt and uncle tonight as they live quite close."

"That's a bit sudden."

"Yes, it is a bit. But it will be worth it."

"It had better be. See you tomorrow night then," she replied abruptly.

"Love ya."

"Ditto," she said, as Geoff had come into the office

and was waiting to speak to her with a slip of paper in his hand.

He stayed for a while talking about a new pig food he wanted to try. James had sanctioned it and he asked her if she could source it as soon as possible. She took the page which he had torn out of a magazine and assured him she would order some this afternoon. He was very enthusiastic in his job and stayed for a while telling her about the benefits of rearing pigs outdoors. He was a nice guy but she was glad when he left as he always carried the aroma of pig with him wherever he went.

The statistics she had been struggling to concentrate on could wait until next week, so she spent a while finding the feed Geoff had asked for at the best rate possible and placed an order.

Back home from work, Chloe was annoyed with Mick as they were meant to be meeting up with Pete and Karen at the pub for a drink and have a game of darts if the bar wasn't too crowded. At a loose end, she rang a couple of friends to see what they were doing this evening, but they were both busy. She knew she could still hook up with Karen and Pete but really didn't want to play the spare part.

Unable to summon up any enthusiasm for cooking she found some crisps and a hunk of cheese and sat down with her iPad and logged on to play Solitaire; but she soon tired of that and turned to Facebook. She scrolled past a few posts before, unable to find the emoji she wanted, chose a sad little face depicting lonely and wrote Bored, bored, bored as her status.

Within seconds there was a ping, and a message from Linda Simmonds.

"Are you lonely tonight?"

"Yes, and bored."

"Where's the boyfriend?"

"He's had to go to Nottingham to look at a job."

"Pity I live so far away."

"Yes. It might have been good to meet up."

"You should be out and having fun. Perhaps you need to find another boyfriend."

"No. I don't think so."

"Is he romantic? Does he buy you gifts and flowers?"

"Not really - but I love him and he loves me."

"Do you trust him?"

"Yes, of course I do."

"Are you sure he's where he says he is?"

"Yes." Chloe was feeling on the defensive now.

Of course she was sure - wasn't she?

What a strange conversation, she thought as she wondered whether to 'un-friend' this girl. Perhaps she had been drinking. She'd give her the benefit of the doubt this time.

It was unusual for Mick to work so far from home but he had mentioned relations in Nottingham before so why wouldn't he be where he said he was?

The doorbell rang. Perhaps it was Mick after all. She crept down the stairs and peered through the frosted glass. It was Bob from downstairs.

"Hello - sorry to bother you but I have a friend here to visit and I haven't got a cork screw. I usually drink beer but we've got a bottle of wine. Do you have one I could borrow?"

"Of course. I've actually got two so you can have one of them. Think of it as a house warming present." She turned and ran up the stairs to find the corkscrew, and was surprised to find that he had followed her and was standing on the landing.

"Thank you so much." He looked round. "Mick not here then?"

"No. He's had to go away for the night."

"I thought I might be able to ask him about a dripping tap."

"He'll be here tomorrow night. I could ask him to pop and see you then."

"That would be great, thanks," he smiled and turned to go.

"How's the flat coming on?" Chloe asked to be friendly as she followed him downstairs.

"I'm almost there."

"When it went on the market I would have loved to buy it, but it was out of my price bracket. It will be interesting to see what you've done.."

"I don't think I've changed the overall atmosphere of the place. I think you would still like it." He stood on the doorstep looking awkward for a couple of seconds as if waiting for her to speak, then turned and hurried back to his guest.

Chloe closed the door as he walked through his front

door. It would be interesting to see what he had done to the old place, she thought, as she turned the key in the lock.

Saturday morning and Chloe looked out of the window. There was a thick fog obscuring the other side of the road. She hoped the sun would burn through before she had to set off. Just a quick cup of tea and she would grab something to eat later. With a bottle of water from the fridge she picked up her car keys and left the flat. It wouldn't be long before she would be dodging Jeremy at the park.

Throwing the bottle onto the passenger seat, she made herself comfortable and turned the key in the ignition before reversing carefully out into the road. Bob was just about to enter the gateway and waved his arms for her to stop. She wound down the window.

"It looks like you've got a flat tyre." he shouted and pointed to the rear offside wheel.

Chloe pulled on the handbrake and got out to have a look.

"Damn and blast!" she exclaimed.

"Would you like me to change it for you?"

"Oh, it's okay. I'll see if the garage can come out."

"I really don't mind. Pull it back into the drive and I'll soon get it done for you."

"Are you sure?"

"Yes. I did a car maintenance course when I learnt to drive. I had a car of my own before I moved to Holland, but as you can imagine I don't need one there."

"In which case , yes, please. I'm afraid I haven't the first idea - although I can check the oil," she added proudly.

Chloe stood watching and was pleased when the sun came through, chasing away the mist and making such a difference in the temperature.

The job took a while as Bob had a problem unscrewing the nuts but finally the car was set back down on all four wheels and ready to go.

"Thank you so much." Chloe almost hugged him. She looked at her watch. "I won't make it to the park in time."

"Tell you what, why don't you run with me? I was going anyway and have found a bridle path at the edge of the village which meets up with a farm track - it's a really lovely route. Just give me five minutes to get changed and we can get started."

Chloe was a bit taken aback but would really miss her Saturday morning exercise and with the sun beginning to make an appearance she couldn't see how she could refuse.

She posted her car keys through her letterbox and glanced at her phone before putting it in her arm band.

There was a message from Mick. "Total waste of time - tell you later."

Bob was very quick and was soon back and ready to go. "I don't expect I'm up to your standard," he said.

"That's OK. You set the pace."

Chloe soon realised that Bob was more of a jogger than a runner and although the route was a pretty one which she would never have done on her own, she felt a little guilty and uncomfortable with the stilted conversation and was glad when they arrived home.

She swiftly took her leave, telling him that she needed to get changed and go into town for a grocery shop. She would be able to drop the spare wheel into the big tyre depot on this side of town and hopefully they could sort it out while she was shopping. She really did need to get a move on as she was meeting Karen in the cafe at the garden centre this afternoon.

CHAPTER 34

Sunday March 22nd

Mick had arrived in a gloomy mood last night. Although he had enjoyed spending time with his cousin on Friday night, Saturday morning had not been so good as Martin Bishop, who had emailed him about the job, failed to turn up at the site meeting on a derelict plot of land which he had bought. They were to have gone over the plans of a house he was building on which Mick, having been well recommended, would do all the plumbing work.

Even though she had enjoyed a good night's sleep, Chloe was still feeling tired, and had woken with a pounding headache. Today she was taking Mick with her to meet her parents for the first time. She was glad he had already met her sister, who would also be there, so would not feel too overwhelmed.

She had not been on form at badminton on Thursday, and had snapped at Mick when he had called her on his way home from Nottingham yesterday. At least her trip to the garden centre had proved to be fruitful. In an effort to cheer herself up she had bought a large green ceramic bowl full of brightly coloured primulas to put by her front door. She had also found an intricate metal candle holder with three delicate glass bowls each holding a flower-encrusted scented candle, which would make the ideal present for her mother. The assistant had carefully wrapped it in pretty paper with a butterfly design with the addition of a neat pink bow.

With Mick sitting in the passenger seat, carefully looking after the present, they were about to leave when Chloe leapt out and ran back to check that she had locked the door, even though Mick insisted that she had.

"People will think you have OCD," Mick teased her as she proved him right.

Chloe looked hurt as she slid back in beside him, but she knew that she was becoming paranoid about locking the door these days. Driving down the motorway, she determinedly lightened her mood, promising Mick a lovely Sunday roast and her mother's delicious Yorkshire puddings, which were a staple requirement no matter what meat was being eaten. It was always a pleasure to go home and she knew her parents were going to love Mick.

As the door opened, they were greeted by the

delicious aroma of roast lamb, which turned out to be every bit as good as it had smelt. Her mother was delighted with her present and Chloe felt better than she had for days as she saw just how well her parents took to Mick. The conversation flowed so smoothly, it was as though they had all known each other for years.

After a leisurely lunch, Dad took Mick into the lounge to show him his photos, while the girls cleared the table and did the washing up for their mother, who sat at the kitchen table with a glass of port which Alex had brought.

Alex took her sister to the back bedroom they used to share to show her the veil she had decided upon for the big day.

"Oh, it's beautiful. I really like the length, and with the pearl edging you could ask Mum if you could borrow her pearl necklace."

"That's a great idea. That could be my something borrowed for the day."

"How are you having your hair?"

Alex was lucky to have an old school friend who had gone on to become a hairdresser in one of the classier salons in town. "I don't want it up so she's suggested some loose curls and a small French braid across the top of the crown to fix the comb on the veil to. She's coming here on the morning of the wedding to sort our hair out."

Alex held the veil on her head to demonstrate.

"That sounds perfect. I want mine naturally straight though if that's all right with you. I might have it swept away from my face somehow but that's all"

"Whatever you are comfortable with will be fine by me."

"Talking of old school friends, do you remember Linda Hughes? She was in my year."

"I can't recall her. Why?"

"She sent me a friend request on Facebook. She wasn't actually a friend at school but I knew her so accepted her invite anyway. She comes across as a bit odd."

"In what way odd?"

"She asks a lot of personal questions."

"You could always un-friend her."

"No, I think she's okay really - just a bit lonely."

Alex gave her one of her looks so Chloe quickly changed the subject.

"I think we had better go and rescue Mick."

They found their mum sitting with the boys in the living room and they were all chatting happily together.

"Mick was just saying he'd like to see more of the village where you grew up, and I suggested we all go for a walk."

"That's a great idea," Chloe replied.

They returned from their walk with rosy cheeks as a chill breeze had sprung up on the way back. Chloe and Mick stood for a while in the garden, overlooking the village from their elevated position.

"I really like it here. I could imagine living somewhere

like this," he said

"The houses around here are too expensive for the likes of us. None of my school friends can afford to live here now. They've all moved away. Come on." Chloe took Mick's hand and led him into warmth of the kitchen where the table was already laid for afternoon tea.

Although the days had been lengthening slowly since the winter solstice the light was beginning to fade, so after enjoying sandwiches and home-made chocolate cake, Chloe and Mick made their farewells. It had been a wonderful carefree day and all the tension seemed to have vanished into thin air. The couple were in high spirits and sang along to the radio, chatted about their day and were generally happy and relaxed in each other's company.

"Can we pop in to the Fox?" Mick asked as they were leaving the motorway.

"That sounds like the perfect end to a perfect day."

She eventually found a space in the crowded car park of the small village pub. It had turned cold and they were pleased to see an open fire licking at the logs in the hearth as they looked round the homely little bar to find a seat at one of the highly-polished wooden tables, sadly bearing the battle scars of the days when smoking was the norm. Mick noticed that the guest beer at the moment was Cotswold Way, one of his favourites, and Chloe opted for a half of lager shandy. Two local lads were playing darts, and some older regulars were propping up the bar. Mick returned with the drinks and with a couple of bags of cheese and onion crisps between his teeth.

"The lounge must be full if the number of cars outside is anything to go by," he observed looking around him at the scant few in the bar.

The pub was quite popular for its cuisine and the lounge had been knocked through into an adjoining outbuilding, making it much larger and ideal for the eating area.

"They will have been busy at lunch time. I've been reading about their Mother's Day lunch offer." She waved a pamphlet.

"Our lunch was superb and so were your parents. They made me feel so at home. I hope they liked me," he said as he picked up his glass.

"I'm sure they did. Sorry if Dad bored you too much with his photos. It's his new hobby."

"It was good that he wanted to show me."

They didn't stop for another as Chloe was tired from driving and Mick had to be at a property before the clients left for work; so they both agreed that they would have an early night and she drove the last few miles back home, where Mick's van was waiting for him.

She kissed him goodbye and stood watching the van's rear lights until they were just a red glow in the distance. With a contented sigh she walked towards her door, sure that she would sleep well tonight.

The security light flashed on and illuminated the ceramic pot by her door, which had been smashed; its poor flowers uprooted and scattered amongst the compost. Chloe fell to her knees, trying to pick up the fated blooms which had looked so beautiful this morning. Who could have done this? Sobbing, she carefully picked up the primulas and set them to one side before clearing the large pieces of ceramic and throwing them into the wheelie bin. She managed to fish out the black plastic tray, which she had discarded yesterday and gently placed the broken plants into it. She was relieved to find that the door was locked when she inserted her key, and only now realised how cold her hands had become as she mounted the stairs cradling her once perfect blooms.

This was criminal damage, she thought, as she placed the tray on the draining board. She washed her hands in the kitchen sink and watched the water run red from a cut she hadn't noticed. Should she call the police? She doubted they'd turn out for a broken flower pot but with everything else that had been happening recently she would let Willis know about it.

CHAPTER 35

Easter Weekend

With silent phone calls, broken nights and unwanted gifts, Chloe was growing more and more agitated and seemed to have a constant background headache. Mick was on edge too, and thought a change of scene would be good for them both; so he had booked them the Easter weekend away. Having spent many happy holidays in Torbay with his parents as a boy he had chosen a well-reviewed bed and breakfast in Paignton, and he was sure Chloe would enjoy the beautiful countryside in that area of Devon.

It was Good Friday and they had made an early start, so that they were already on the M5 by 6.15am. While Mick drove, Chloe watched the sky change through different hues of pink until the bright orange sun burst onto the horizon behind them. They didn't hit much traffic until they reached Exeter. The forecast for the weekend was good and all the stress of the last few weeks seemed to melt away as each mile passed.

They arrived in Paignton late morning and as they couldn't check in until 2pm, Mick parked up and they made the short walk to the seafront. They strolled along the promenade as far as the beach huts and back, before relishing fish and chips at a restaurant looking out over the sea and sand. They watched a persistent seagull eventually peck its way into a carrier bag and start to eat the binned contents of someone's sandwiches.

"It's different to how I remember it here," Mick sighed, as they walked hand in hand back up the main street, where paint was peeling on the fascias of the many gift shops. The whole place looked tired. "It seems like no one cares anymore."

The road where the B&B was situated looked no better from the van as they drove round to book in, but they were pleasantly surprised when they drew up outside the house.

"Wow!" Chloe exclaimed as they walked through the open gate which was set in a wall covered in tumbling purple aubrietia. The borders were packed with forget-me-nots, daffodils, bright red tulips and bright pink anemones.

Mick rang the doorbell and they were welcomed by the lady of the house, who showed them to the top floor. She explained that they had spent the winter upgrading the two rooms on this floor and hoped they would enjoy their stay. The room was tastefully decorated in shades of peach and grey and looked out over the back garden, where bedding swayed lazily on the line, one end of which was attached to an apple tree covered in pink-tinged blossom.

"It's perfect," Chloe told Mick with a smile that he hadn't seen for some weeks.

Saturday morning, and after a full English breakfast, Chloe and Mick were near the front of the queue for the bus to Totnes. Mick was disappointed that it wasn't an open-topped one as shown on the brochure, but as it was only April he realised that the weather could be too changeable. They managed to get a pair of front seats and settled down to watch the fields roll past. The sun was shining and Chloe thought it wouldn't be long before they would be carrying the jackets they were wearing. An elderly couple seated behind them were telling a young family that they were celebrating their golden wedding anniversary.

Chloe remarked on this when they were walking along the river at Totnes. "How sweet to have been together for fifty years and to come back to the place where they spent their honeymoon."

Mick squeezed her hand and saw her use the other to wipe away an emotional tear.

They came to a bridge which they crossed to stroll up a hill which was they decided must be the high street of the quaint little town, with its bakers and butchers and other independent shops dotted between the more well known stores.

"This place has got such character," Chloe said.

She glanced up at the clock on the arch which spanned the road. It was time they made their way back to the riverside to continue their excursion by boat down the river Dart.

Although most of the other passengers had boarded when they arrived, there were still plenty of seats on the top deck, and they didn't have to wait long before they were on their way.

"Look - a seal!" Chloe pointed as a sleek dog-like head popped up from the water.

"Wow! And there's another. I'm surprised to see them so far upstream."

The tour guide saw them too, and told them that it was quite common to see seals as far up the river as Totnes and that they should look out for others on the way.

It was a leisurely cruise down the river with an interesting and often humorous commentary. Mick seemed in a world of his own as he relaxed and took in the sights.

They arrived at Dartmouth and climbed the steps up from the jetty, then turned left and walked hand in hand along the wide riverside path. A light breeze jangled the rigging of the dozens of little boats which bobbed at anchor on the tide and Mick pointed out the castle round the cove. A little boy walked by clutching a soft ice cream. Chloe quickly found the source and steered Mick to the edge of the road.

"I can take a hint," he smiled. "Would you like an ice cream?"

"Ooh yes - can I have a flake too?"

"Of course you can."

They crossed the road to the ice cream parlour and were amazed at how many flavours there were to choose from. It was several minutes before they wandered back to find a bench from where they could enjoy the view.

"This is wonderful. It must be the sea air making me feel so good. Thank you so much for bringing me." Chloe kissed Mick on the cheek and laughed when she realised she had left a rum and raisin flavoured mark.

Mick looked serious as he fiddled in his pocket to get a tissue but he surprised her when he carefully unfolded it and held out a small box, which he opened to reveal a dainty diamond ring.

"Chloe, I love you, and I want to spend the rest of my life with you. Will you marry me?"

She threw her arms round him. "Yes! Oh, yes!"

He put the ring on her finger. Blinking back tears of happiness, Chloe held her hand out to admire the effect. "It's lovely, but it's a little bit loose. I'm scared I'll lose it.

Mick hurried to reassure her. "The jeweller said we can have it resized. Best not to wear it until then."

With one last look, she slid it over her knuckle and replaced it in its box which she tucked securely into a little zipped compartment in her handbag. She reached up for a lingering kiss. "The next time I put it on, it will stay there," she promised him. "It feels like things are finally coming right for us."

"We've lost a bit of time, with one thing and another, and I just couldn't wait any longer. Let's get married soon, eh?""

The rest of the afternoon went by quickly in a mixture of sightseeing and making plans. They took the ferry boat to Kingswear before catching the steam train back to Paignton, sleepy and a little sunburnt, and feeling very much in love. They gazed out in silence at the beautiful scenery and the wonderful glimpses of the peaceful blue sea. All too soon the engine puffed into the station.

"It's been a lovely day," Chloe said as they walked along the promenade.

Mick smiled and kissed her on the forehead.

"I'm so glad you said yes."

"I'm so excited – I can't wait to tell everyone about our engagement."

"Me too."

"It would be so much better to tell our parents in person than to phone them. Do you think we could pop in to see mine on the way home?"

"I think that's an excellent idea."

They crossed the road to head inland to where their accommodation stood.

There was no one about as they unlocked the front door so they were able to go straight up to their room where they fell onto the bed in each other's arms.

Some time later Mick announced that rather than

find a pub for their meal tonight they should go out and celebrate. He got up and started to leaf through the pamphlets that had been left for guests in a unit on the dressing table.

"How do you fancy tapas?" he asked.

"I loved tapas when I went to Spain some years ago."

"Well, there's a restaurant called Olive near the harbour. I'll see if I can book a table."

A phone call later they had a reservation for 8pm.

A quick shower and a change of clothes and they were on their way. It didn't take long to find the restaurant.

The food was wonderful and they opted for a bottle of cava to enjoy with it.

"Here's to us," Mick said as he raised his glass.

"To us!"

Seagulls provided a rather early wake-up call from the roof of a block of flats.

"Are you awake?" Mick asked.

"Yep. I've been listening to the seaside's version of the dawn chorus."

Chloe rolled over and pressed her body against his. Mick didn't need any more encouragement and they enjoyed each other's bodies as they celebrated their new relationship status.

After a late breakfast they retraced their steps from the following evening to the harbour and found the signpost which indicated a coastal walk. When they reached the parkland at the top of the first ascent they met a brisk breeze coming in from the sea; Mick put a protective arm around Chloe and drew her close. She smiled and kissed the end of his nose.

The pathway snaked down through gardens on the steep hillside, and they found a good vantage point from which to watch the spume from the waves crashing onto rocks below.

"I love the sea in all its different moods," Chloe said.

"I love the sound too. It's never silent."

They continued along the path as it zig-zagged down towards Goodrington Sands, where Chloe pointed ahead to a large, white-painted building with a quirky grey-slate roof. A turret to the left and gable windows to the right suggested it had once been a group of different houses. "I saw that pub from the train yesterday. I wonder if we could get some lunch there later."

As they drew closer, they found a sign outside indicating that booking was advisable for Sunday lunch, so Mick popped inside to reserve a table.

A little further on there was a park where swan-shaped boats were moored up on a small lake, and a few children were running around a playground.

"I expect this would be really busy in the summer. Such a lovely place to bring children," Chloe mused.

"Perhaps we will bring ours one day," Mick grinned.

"That won't be for a while," she said, punching him playfully.

"No, although I would like children sometime in the future."

"So would I, but we have a wedding to arrange first."

He looked at her a little uncertainly. "I'd really like a small ceremony with close family and a few friends."

Chloe smiled, giving his arm a comforting squeeze. "That is exactly what I'd like too."

They kissed and, hand in hand, returned to the coastal path, which climbed upwards beyond the town. As the track changed from gravel to grass, the whistle of a steam train announced its approach on the railway below. They waited until it chugged past leaving a trail of smoke and steam in its wake, then carried on for another mile or so.

Chloe checked her watch. "We'd better turn back, or we'll be late for lunch."

After a very pleasant meal, washed down with a pint of Doom Bar ale, they wandered back to Paignton. They had intended to have a last Devon cream tea but were still too full from lunch, so instead they found a bench on the seafront to watch the brave souls helping their children to build sandcastles on the beach.

It was Easter Monday all too soon. After breakfast they packed the van and set off towards home. It was a smooth run and they left the M5 at junction 10 to make the short drive to call on Chloe's parents, who were overjoyed at the news. Chloe's dad was relieved to hear that they intended to wait a while before getting married so that they could save up a good deposit on a house. He too would have to start saving. There was a lot to talk about and the couple stayed rather longer than they had intended, so it was getting late when they arrived back at Chloe's flat. They had intended to call in to tell his parents too, but decided to wait until tomorrow night, and Chloe promised that she wouldn't breathe a word to anyone until they had.

"I need to fill up with fuel on the way home so I won't come in," Mick said as he carried her suitcase to her door.

"Thank you for such a wonderful weekend." Chloe held her fiancé tightly, not really wanting to let him go.

Mick looked at her and grinned. "It was good, wasn't it?"

Still smiling, and without a care in the world Chloe put the key into her lock and turned to wave him goodbye.

The heat hit her as soon as she opened the door to the landing. She was certain she had turned the heating off before leaving on Friday. She strode straight through into the kitchen to check the heating settings on the boiler and found that instead of turning it off she had switched it to high. How had she managed to do something so stupid? She shut it down now and opened the window. When she went to put the clotted cream she had bought this morning into the fridge she found the door was ajar. It sometimes didn't catch if it wasn't closed hard enough and she usually checked. Luckily there wasn't much in there, and apart from a rather smelly piece of ham, the rest seemed ok. She could only assume she had, as usual, been in too much of a hurry to set off.

Her stress levels were already beginning to creep up.

CHAPTER 36

Friday May 1st

Chloe was late leaving work as the afternoon hadn't gone according to plan. The demonstration and talk to a class of eager year five children had been delayed when one of them needed first aid on a badly grazed knee. Just as she was about to pack up, a phone call from a scout group asking about a weekend camp at the farm delayed her even further.

Finally the weekend was here, and her first job when she got home was to open the kitchen window. There had been a nasty smell in there for a few days now and she hadn't been able to find what was causing it. She had been through the fridge and the cupboards and cleaned every surface but still it remained. A large fly buzzed past her ear as she put a bottle of white wine into the fridge ready for tomorrow when Karen was coming round. She opened the window further and managed to encourage the persistent insect to leave with the aid of a tea towel grabbed hastily from the oven rail.

It had been a gloriously warm week and she and Mick planned to sit out in the large beer garden at the Kings Arms with a drink and a bar snack to watch the canal boats. He was due soon so she changed into a comfortable pair of jeans and tee shirt and took a cardigan from the wardrobe in case it turned chilly later.

The pub was doing a roaring trade so they had to wait a while for their scampi and chips.

"I almost bought a canal boat once," Chloe said, watching a particularly well-painted one glide past.

Mick's eyebrows shot up. "Really? Why?"

"I fancied the idea of living on one. Probably too cramped for everyday life, but I wouldn't mind a canal holiday, just drifting from place to place, and mooring up at a different pub every night."

"That sounds more like it," he agreed.

Back at Chloe's flat, a big black fly buzzed past them the moment she opened the kitchen door.

"There was one in here earlier," Chloe remarked, batting it away with the palm of her hand.

Mick grabbed a fish slice from the utensil jar and whacked at it but missed as it flew out towards the living room. He followed it and finally despatched it against the window pane. Within seconds there was another fly buzzing around the room.

With a second fly sent packing out through the kitchen window Chloe turned on the TV and they settled down to watch the news.

It wasn't long before another two flies were buzzing loudly round the room.

"Where are they coming from?" Chloe asked.

"The first one was in the kitchen so maybe we should start by looking there." Mick jumped up and encountered another as he walked into the kitchen. "They may be coming through the air brick, or there may be a dead mouse somewhere. We had one once that died behind one of the cupboards. It could explain the smell there's been recently."

"How can we find out?"

"We'll have to move all the furniture, look under the units and drag out the washing machine and fridge freezer." Mick rolled up his sleeves and started hauling the washing machine out enough to peer behind, while Chloe found a torch to look under the units.

She removed everything from the top of the fridge freezer and Mick gradually inched it forwards into the middle of the room. There, against the skirting board, was what looked like the slimy remains of a blackbird and a few drowsy looking flies nearby.

Chloe heaved as Mick threw the creature out of the window, which faced onto a scruffy patch of land at the side of the property. He swept the newly hatched flies up with a dustpan and brush and flung them out too, quickly closing the window behind them. Chloe fetched a bucket of soapy water and together they scrubbed the residue.

"Poor thing must have been there for some time," Chloe reasoned, "and I have no idea how it could have got in. I never leave windows open when I'm not here."

"Perhaps it flew in while you were out of the room."

"I only open them when I'm in here cooking to stop the panes steaming up."

"Well, it must have got in somehow when you weren't looking."

Chloe shuddered.

"I wonder if it had a disease or something. I saw a dead one in the garden a few weeks ago and thought at the time it must have been killed by a cat."

Another fly buzzed noisily around their heads before heading onto the landing where it buzzed angrily against the ceiling tantalising out of reach.

There were two more in the living room. Mick killed one with a rolled up magazine but the other went to ground.

"I've just remembered something. I'd stupidly switched the heating to high instead of off before we were away at Easter and it was stiflingly hot when I got home. I opened all the windows then to help cool the place down."

Mick thought it highly unlikely that it had come in during the night but decided it was best not to voice the alternative which came to mind.

While Chloe took a shower, Mick prowled around making sure there were no more flies lurking about. It was pitch dark by the time he clambered into bed.

Just the thought of the flies was enough to keep Chloe awake for some time as she imagined them finding a way into her bedroom and crawling in her hair. She must have eventually nodded off in the small hours. When daylight crept around the curtain she was awake again, ears strained, as she waited for her boyfriend to wake up.

Sending him out of the room first, she was relieved when he shouted back to her that there didn't seem to be any more unwelcome visitors.

CHAPTER 37

Wednesday May 27th

It was a bright evening and the sun shone warmly through the windscreen as Chloe drove to Forest-in-the-Green to collect the bridesmaid's dresses which she would take with her to her parents' home in the morning. The cow parsley had grown abundantly over the past couple of weeks and stood in white frothy clouds on the verges. A hot air balloon sailed serenely over the nearby fields and a cuckoo's call from the valley below floated through the open window. She had asked Karen if she would like to go for a walk down by the river and she had readily agreed, offering to pick her up once she had taken the dresses home.

The fragrant scent of a mock orange filled the air as she approached Karen's parents' house.

Mrs Reynolds met her at the door. "You take your

dress and I'll follow with the other. I bought a couple of covers to keep them clean, but I'll have them back sometime, if that's okay."

"That's great, thank you." Chloe took the dress and carried it to her car.

"The weather is set to be grand for the rest of the week so your sister should have a splendid day for her wedding."

"Yes, it should be wonderful." Chloe gently placed her dress onto the back seat before taking Becky's dress and laying it on top.

"Thank you so much for making these. They're absolutely beautiful."

"It was a pleasure."

Chloe rang Karen to say she was leaving and started off towards home. On arrival she decided to leave the dresses where they were, as she would be leaving early in the morning, and stood by her car, enjoying the sunshine while she waited for her friend. Karen wasn't far behind her and beeped her horn from the road and they were soon on their way.

It was an ideal evening to be out in the fresh air and the girls chatted happily as they wandered along the riverside. The frothy, white flowers of the meadowsweet smelt divine and they had a rare sighting of a water vole as it swam towards the far bank. Towards nine, as the sun put on a glorious show in bright shades of red and orange on the western horizon, a chilly breeze blew up so they hurried back to where they had left the car and headed to Chloe's for a coffee.

A dark green car was parked up at the other side of the road, making it difficult for Karen to manoeuvre into the drive, so she pulled in behind it. Chloe wondered if it was the same one she had seen there before but didn't say anything. Her friend would think she was completely paranoid.

It was past ten when Karen left and Chloe locked the door behind her, as she bounded back upstairs to pack the last minute things ready for her early departure the next day.

CHAPTER 38

Thursday May 28th

Bright sunlight was already streaming through a crack in the curtains lighting up the dust motes as they danced in the breeze from the open window. Chloe had woken to the high pitched twitter of house martins filling the air as they swooped into their intricately made nests in the eaves. She had not slept well; but then, she had forgotten the last time she had slept the whole night through.

There was no bread left for toast so she used the last bit of milk in the bottle to have a bowl of cornflakes before double-checking that everything was turned off. She would keep to the A roads this morning as the motorway would be busy with lorries and commuters, and could enjoy a more leisurely drive to Gloucestershire.

Just after Wellesbourne she was delighted to see masses of cowslips on the wide grass verges. A childhood favourite, she would pick big bunches of them in the fields, and they always brought back happy memories of growing up with her sister.

Her phone began to ring as she reached the railway bridge at Moreton-in-Marsh and she answered it on hands-free. It was Pete.

"Chloe, I've been trying your house phone. Where are you?"

"On my way to my parents' house. Why?"

"Did Karen stay with you last night?"

"No. She left soon after ten."

"She didn't come home."

"Oh. I'm sure there is some simple explanation. She was tired when she left. Perhaps she went to her mother's as it's nearer."

"I've been trying to get hold of her but her phone is switched off. I thought she must still be with you, but when I didn't get an answer on your landline I waited a good hour before ringing you now in case she was on her way home. I just don't know where she can be."

"Try her mum. If she's not there, perhaps call the police."

"I will. Thanks." Pete hung up.

A sudden shiver engulfed Chloe as a fluffy white cloud obscured the sun. She thought about last night and how Karen had left in good spirits to drive home. What could have happened to change her plans and why hadn't she called Pete?

Deep in thought, Chloe missed her turning off the Fosseway and had to find a gateway to turn round in. Once she was back on track it wasn't long before she was parking up in the drive of her parental home.

Her mother was watering the flower borders in the shady front garden and Chloe realised that she had forgotten to water her tubs before leaving this morning. The pansies which she had bought to replace the flowers wrecked in the mindless vandal attack would be dry and shrivelled by the time she got home on Sunday night. When she phoned Mick later she would ask him to pop round and water them for her tonight once the sun had started to lose its heat.

"I've nearly finished here. We'll have some coffee when I come in." Her mum put down the watering can and hugged her. "Dad's in the front room struggling with his speech for tomorrow."

Chloe wandered through to find her father sitting at his bureau surrounded by scraps of scrunched-up paper.

"Hello, darling." He got up, took her in his arms and planted a kiss on her forehead. "Did you have a good journey?"

"Yes, I came by the scenic route. Everything is looking so fresh and green at the moment," she told him. "I can see you're busy, so I'll go and fetch my case."

"I could do with a break from this," he indicated the A4 pad on the desk. "I'll come and help you."

Together they wandered out to the car, where Chloe opened the boot for her dad to lift out the suitcase. She followed upstairs to her old bedroom with the dresses and hung them on the hook inside the door. She looked round at her room which was exactly as she remembered it, except for the lack of clutter. She sat on the end of the bed and found herself staring into the large mirror on top of the chest of drawers, and was taken aback at the drawn, tired face that she saw there.

She was worried about Karen, and was wondering if she should try to phone her when her father's voice drifted up the stairs.

"Coffee's ready."

"Coming." After taking a couple of minutes to compose herself, she ran down to the comfort of her mother's kitchen.

There was coffee but also a china plate with a slice of home-made Victoria sponge waiting for her on the kitchen table, where her parents were already seated.

"Alex will be arriving later and I've booked a table for the four of us at the local tonight," her dad announced before taking a sip of his drink.

"What would you like to do until Alex gets here?" her mum asked.

"I'd love to go for a walk across the fields. Would anyone like to join me?"

"I still have this blessed speech to finish. What about you, Sandra?"

"I'll come with you. Just give me a chance to get changed out of these rags."

"I have a couple of phone calls to make then we can go, if that's all right?"

"That should give me plenty of time."

Chloe made the calls from her room. First she tried Karen's number and found it to be switched off. Then she rang Pete who answered almost immediately.

"Have you heard from Karen yet?" she asked.

"No. I'm so worried, Chloe. Her mother hasn't heard from her either. She can't just vanish. I rang the police and they took some details"

"You've got me worried too. If she gets in touch, please tell her to ring me."

"I will."

"Promise?"

"Yes - I promise."

Chloe found her mother, changed and ready, casually dead-heading the scented white rose which clambered up the porch trellis by the back door, and they started off along the lane to where the footpath began.

"Are you all right?" her mum asked. "It's just that you look so pale and tired."

"I'm fine, Mum. I'm worried about my friend, actually. We spent the evening together yesterday, and she set off just after ten, but Pete, her boyfriend, rang this morning to say no-one's seen her. She seemed perfectly happy when she left me and hadn't mentioned any problems. I can't imagine what could have happened to her."

CHAPTER 39

Friday May 29th

The big day started early with the arrival of the hairdresser and Chloe just had time to text Mick to ask him what time he would be there before throwing herself into helping her mum with last minute items and the important job of applying her sister's makeup. It was late morning when she picked up her mobile to find a text - not from Mick as she had expected, but from Pete. The police had found Karen's car in a cul-de-sac near to where Chloe lived. She tried to phone Mick, but there was no answer so she dialled Pete's number, also to no avail. She left messages for both of them to call her and went to join the others. Dad had just popped a bottle of champagne and she forced a smile as she took the glass she was offered.

"Today is such a happy day for us all. Alexandra, we

wish you every joy in the new life you will start today. To your happiness."

"To your happiness." Everyone raised their glass.

With the vicar, groom and best man in their places, the congregation stood as the organ struck up the unmistakeable first chords of the Wedding March. Sandra Thornby, in the front pew, clutching a crumpled tissue, watched proudly as the slim auburn-haired bride was escorted in through the sturdy oak door of the small private church by her father, closely followed by her two bridesmaids.

Brenda Hartley accidently knocked her son's arm as she turned to get a first look at the bride, making him drop the order of service he was holding, and he dived down to recover it. He was already grumpy and hadn't wanted to come. It was half term so he'd had no excuse. He hadn't kept in touch with Giles; they had gone their different ways when they started secondary school. His mind was miles away as he stared blindly at the stained glass windows behind the altar. On auto-pilot, he stood when everyone else did and pretended to sing while studying the blurred words on the card in front of him.

Chloe, holding tightly to the posy of delicate yellow roses, could have done with a tissue when her eyes began to well up as her sister said her vows. She was sad, too, that her beloved Mick hadn't been able to make it in time for the service. In an effort to stem the tears, she stared at a painting on the wall depicting the country estate in spring with brightly coloured flowers and sheep grazing in the distance and with the church at its centre. With time to think she started worrying about her friend too. Where was Karen? What had happened to her?

While the register was signed in the tiny vestry, the congregation listened to a recording of Vivaldi's Four Seasons, which continued playing as the bride and groom led the rest of the congregation from the cool interior of the church into bright sunshine. The guests were encouraged to pass through the ornate black metal gate at the side of the churchyard to take a walk in the extensive grounds while they waited for the photographer to take the group pictures.

Brenda was in her element and chattered happily as she and Robin passed the small duck pond, where a female mallard dashed out from the yellow flag irises and swam away noisily. So enthralled was she with the grounds that it wasn't until she spotted the vintage Rolls Royce cruising sedately up the tree-lined drive towards the house that she realised just how quiet her son was.

"Come on, it's time we headed for the big house," she informed him.

Completely in a world of his own, Robin didn't seem to hear her. Brenda clapped her hands to get his attention. He jumped and looked shocked as if he didn't even know where he was.

"Are you okay?" she enquired.

"Yes. Sorry. Well, I have got a bit of a headache. I

think I'll go and sit in the car for a while. Come and get me when the reception is about to begin."

With that he left her and headed to the small field on the other side of the drive which had been allotted as the car park for today. He was glad that he had parked under the shade of a mature oak tree.

Brenda felt self conscious as she walked up the drive along with other guests in their couples and groups. The only person she knew was Diane who was far too busy today, so she accepted the offered glass of Pimms from the smartly dressed waiter and took herself off to a seat in the garden under a bower of sweet-smelling honeysuckle. Feeling less conspicuous here she settled down to watch the other guests in all their finery, as they mingled and chatted. Every now and then a waitress would appear with a silver tray of canapés for her to choose from, a dainty pastry, perhaps, or a cherry tomato stuffed with cream cheese. The sun was warm and bees hummed in the abundant floral heaven.

Awakened from her reverie as a dinner gong sounded, Brenda placed her glass on the white-painted metal table and headed for the car park to find her son. He was sitting in the driving seat with the windows open and looking at his mobile phone. As her approaching shadow darkened the rear window he quickly put the phone away.

"Are you feeling better now?" she enquired. "The gong has rung and people have started to go indoors."

He shut the car up and accompanied her for the short walk to the gardens where they joined the queue of people weaving towards the doorway of the magnificent Victorian building. They filed slowly into a splendid room where tables were set up ready for the wedding breakfast and the bride and groom were waiting with their parents to greet them, and then moved on to the display board to discover where they would be seated.

Having arrived with the bridal party, Chloe and Becky left their posies on a table in the corner beside the wedding cake as they had been instructed, and wandered round to find their allotted places. Chloe left Becky to sit with her parents and then settled at a round table for eight near the top table. Mick's place was set next to hers but so far Chloe had seen nothing of him. When she had spoken to him last night he had told her that he would be staying with his mate to keep him company. Despite leaving the message on his phone earlier he hadn't called her back. Maybe he hadn't seen her text. Surely he was on his way and would be here soon. She hadn't said anything to Alex as she didn't want to spoil her day. She would try phoning again once she could retrieve her mobile from her mother's handbag.

Gazing around at the guests as they took their seats she was surprised to see someone staring at her - a guy wearing black-rimmed Michael Caine style glasses and a rather out-dated suit. He looked oddly familiar but she didn't think she actually knew him. She wished that Mick would hurry or the meal would be starting without him.

Two couples came and sat at her table and she recognised the girls as old school friends of her sister. They all made small talk for a while and a third couple arrived just before they were all invited to stand up as the bride and groom walked to the top table.

A flurry of waitresses began bringing the first course. As Chloe waited for her plate she looked towards the door in the hope of seeing Mick hurrying in. Bitterly disappointed, she realised the man she had noticed earlier was still staring at her. He smiled shyly when he realised she had seen him and slowly looked away to speak to the older woman by his side. Honeydew melon with Parma ham was placed in front of Chloe and she had to force herself to eat it while her mind raced. Something was very wrong. Mick should be there. Why wasn't he answering his phone? Had he had an accident? Where was he?

When everyone had finished their starter and chatting re-commenced, Chloe realised that the girl who had arrived last at the table with her fiancé, judging from the diamond solitaire on her left hand, was Marie Johnson from their village. She introduced her 'other half' as Jim Bolton. The polite conversation soon dried up. Desperate to phone her boyfriend, Chloe excused herself to discreetly ask her mother for her phone.

"Where's Mick got to?" her mother hissed as she handed over the Samsung.

"I don't know. I'm really worried."

She walked out into the entrance hall and tried his

number, which yet again went through to answerphone, and she sent a quick text before returning to the reception. Having to pass a few tables to get back to her place she was rewarded with a huge grin from the strange man and forced a curt smile in response. Her mother gave her a questioning look as she passed and she shook her head in reply.

During the main course, the talk at the table was of school days. Alex's friends were chatting about what they used to get up to with the bride and Marie asked Chloe where she was living now and what she was doing, slipping in a question about the empty chair next to Chloe. She told them enthusiastically about her job at the animal farm and explained that her boyfriend had been delayed and would be coming later.

Chloe picked at the coq au vin which she would have usually enjoyed, and accepted another glass of Chardonnay, which was starting to go to her head. Marie leant over and whispered, "Robin Hartley can't keep his eyes off of you," and discreetly pointed in the direction of the strange man. Chloe blushed as she followed Marie's direction, and found that he was still looking at her.

"Oh, crumbs! He used to have a crush on me when we were at school. He asked me out once. But that can't be Robin Hartley," she exclaimed. "It doesn't look anything like him."

"It is. He lost a lot of weight when he went to university and is now a teacher at a local primary school."

Chloe's phone sang out to alert her of a text message.

"At last!" she muttered as she saw it was from Mick.

"Sorry. It's over. I love Karen and I'm with her now."

Chloe's hand flew to her mouth and she walked as quickly as she could out of the room, out of the building and into the garden where she found a seat in an alcove where she could read the text again.

She typed back "Why?" and waited. Nothing. Too shocked even to cry, she sat staring at the lilac blooms of the wisteria which climbed the wall next to her. There had been no signs; both he and Karen had seemed perfectly normal. Surely this must be a joke. After all, Mick had only just asked her to marry him; but Karen had vanished, and he hadn't arrived. Perhaps it wasn't a coincidence.

Knowing that she would be missed, she took a deep breath and went back indoors where she helped herself to a good swig of wine in an effort to calm herself down. At least someone there seemed to find her attractive. She raised her glass in his direction and smiled. Determined to put Michael Benfield to the back of her mind she attacked the sherry trifle with gusto.

The speeches followed and Chloe, emotional and a bit light-headed, decided it would be prudent to slow down a bit and sip the champagne for the toasts.

Not knowing anyone else, Marie's boyfriend was obviously getting bored and he took his phone out of his jacket pocket and began to scroll on it under the table.

"Can't you just give it a break for one afternoon?" Marie asked through gritted teeth before announcing to the whole table that her fiancé was a mobile phone addict. He happily agreed that he was.

"Are you on any social media, Chloe?" she asked.

"Just on Facebook - but I only look at it at specific times of the day."

"I just can't see the point in it," Marie huffed.

"It's a good way of keeping in touch with old friends. For example I've recently made friends with Linda Hughes, though it's not Hughes now. I can't remember her married name. We chat quite often although sometimes she seems a bit strange - but then she always was," she smiled.

Marie looked aghast. "Linda? Well, that's just not possible."

"What do you mean? Of course it is - are you calling me a liar?" Chloe was becoming annoyed with this girl's attitude.

"Well, no," Marie looked uncomfortable, "only you can't communicate with the dead. She died in a car crash - it must have been two years ago."

"But - you must be mistaken." Chloe was lost for words and grabbed her phone to prove her point. Finding her profile she showed the others at the table.

"It sounds as if her account must have been hacked and someone else has stolen her identity," Jim said.

"She only contacted me a few months ago," Chloe replied

She hadn't thought of her stalker for a few days and

this brought him straight to the front of her mind. She shuddered as she realised that, if this was him, he would have been receiving her posts and knew where she would be, what she was doing - everything she had posted. It still didn't tell her who he was - but it might help the police.

She clicked "unfriend" next to Linda's name. At least she knew her stalker couldn't have followed her here as she'd not mentioned the wedding at her sister's request.

Coffee and chocolate mints were distributed to the tables and the photographer took this opportunity to escort the bride and groom into the garden to get some good shots by the ornamental fish pond, pink rose-covered pergola and the ornate wishing well.

Soon all the guests were invited to enjoy some time out in the gardens, where a little band would entertain them while the room could be transformed for the evening reception. Chloe picked up her glass, which someone had filled when she wasn't looking, and wandered out to find her family, who had taken over a big table on the patio near to the orangery.

"What's happened to Mick?" her mother asked.

"His van broke down," she lied. " He won't be coming."

"Oh, what a shame. Such a nice lad. Dad and I were looking forward to seeing him again."

Chloe concentrated on watching Alex and Giles as they posed for yet another photo under the pergola. They looked so happy. She had thought that she and

Mick were happy too. What had gone wrong?
The DJ announced the first dance was about to begin and invited the bride and groom to take to the floor. The soothing voice of Ed Sheeran sang of love under a starlit sky. Chloe sat and watched the happy couple dancing together, looking into each other's eyes and so obviously in love. It brought tears which she couldn't hold back any longer. She quietly walked out through the door beside her and ran to a more secluded part of the garden.

The tears were falling down her cheeks when Robin found her.

"A pretty girl like you shouldn't be sat outside all by herself. Can I sit with you?"

Chloe shrugged and peered through the thick lenses into his steel grey eyes.

"Oh, my love, why are you crying?" he reached into his pocket and handed her a handkerchief.

"Please leave me. I need to spend some time on my own. I'll be back indoors once I've tidied up."

"Come and talk to me when you do." He gave her a long, concerned look before walking away slowly.

Not wanting anyone else to find her in this state she scurried to the ladies, which fortunately was empty. With her make-up repaired and feeling more confident, Chloe walked back to join the evening reception and looked around for Robin who was seated at the far side next to what must be his mother. She would prefer not to talk to him so made her way to find her parents, who were with her aunt and uncle.

"Where did you get to?" her mother greeted her.

"I just needed some fresh air."

"I've told Alex about Mick. Such a shame. Giles was looking forward to meeting him."

There was a tap on Chloe's shoulder and she turned round to find Robin standing right behind her.

"Would you like to dance?"

All the years disappeared and Chloe felt as horrified as she had all those years ago when he had asked her to go out with him. She looked past the man before her to the boy he once was. Her face probably said it all as she took a pace backwards.

"I prefer something a bit more upbeat to dance to," she stuttered.

Robin looked surprised and embarrassed. "Maybe later," he muttered as he quickly went over to his mother, said something to her, and together they left the room.

Chloe heard the unmistakable ring tone of her phone and took it from her clutch bag. It was Pete. He must know of Karen's infidelity, she thought, when she saw his number.

"Hi Chloe. I've still not heard from Karen and now Mrs Benfield has been on the phone, worried sick, she says she hasn't seen Mick since yesterday evening. His suit is still hung up on the back of his bedroom door."

"Pete, you aren't going to like this but... Mick has broken up with me by text and says he is with Karen now."

"That's impossible. He wouldn't do that to me. He

wouldn't do that to you either."

"Well, he has, Pete, and I'm as shocked as you."

"I don't believe it. I'm going to ring the police." Pete rang off, leaving Chloe feeling even more confused that she already did.

If the suit was ready then he must have been intending to wear it. She dialled DI Willis, whose number she had saved in her contacts.

CHAPTER 40

Saturday May 30th

Chloe hadn't slept a wink and was up early and ready to go. Her mother was upset that she wasn't staying another night and refused breakfast.

"Are you sure? Not even a bacon sandwich?"

"I'm really sorry, Mum, but I need to get back." She kissed her on the cheek, grabbed her small suitcase and hurried to her car. No scenic route today; she would soon be heading north on the M5 to the police station at Forest-in-the-Green.

"I've come to see DI Willis," she announced at the front desk.

The constable on duty phoned through before asking her to accompany him. They took the stairs to the first floor and she was shown into a bright, airy office where two men were sitting at desks.

Willis rose and introduced his colleague, DCI Green.

"Take a seat," he said. "So you think something may have happened to your boyfriend."

"Yes. He was supposed to join me at my sister's wedding yesterday but he didn't show up. Then out the blue I had a text to say that we were through and that he was with Karen now. My friend Karen went missing after she left me on Wednesday evening."

"So why do you think something has happened to him?"

"Well, apart from the fact that he has only recently asked me to marry him," she said, "It's just not the way he would phrase it." She took her phone out and showed him the text.

"Certainly short and to the point," Willis mused.

"After all the strange things that have happened over the past few months I'm convinced it has something to do with my stalker and the threats to Mick."

"Have there been some more developments?"

"No but... I've told you about things that I received from the stalker but there have been some strange events that I didn't think had anything to do with him. Now, maybe I think they were."

"What sort of things?" Willis had his pen poised.

"My ceramic plant pot of flowers, which I had only bought the day before, was smashed while Mick and I were visiting my mum for Mother's Day."

"What else?"

"Little things, like the heating being on full blast when I got back from a weekend away; a dead blackbird behind the fridge; a dark green car parked across the road."

"Slow down. I think you need to write all these down for me. Do you leave a window open when you are out?"

"No, never."

"You would lock the front door, so is there any other way anyone could enter your flat when you are out - a roof-light maybe?"

"No." Chloe blushed - she felt silly now.

"Have you given anyone else a key - a member of your family or a friend?"

"No. Not even Mick has a key."

Willis wondered if the boyfriend had tired of the situation, and he thought there was probably another explanation for the rest, but he handed her the pad from his desk.

"I'll take you to a quiet office. I want you to write down all the strange things that have happened and, if you can, when. Exact dates would be good, if you know them. Would you like a drink?"

"Yes, please. I would love a cup of tea, milk, one sugar."

"I'll have one brought to you. I have to go out so when you've finished, hand your list in at the main desk."

Left alone, Chloe tried to remember everything from the scratch to Mr Benfield's car, which they had later realised had been caused by a key being scraped along the door, to the fake social media account. She didn't write about the feeling she sometimes had that there was someone in the flat at night because there clearly wasn't, and he would think she was crazy. When she had finished she handed it in as instructed and headed home.

Diane was feeling like a lost soul today after all the excitement of the wedding yesterday. It had been a lovely day and Giles' new in-laws seemed a very pleasant couple. Today was proving to be a real anti-climax. She was in the kitchen with the large piece of cake which Mrs Thornton - Sandra - had given her yesterday as she wanted to send some to a couple of elderly relations who hadn't been able to make it to the festivities. She was thinking of taking a slice round to Brenda as she and her son had left before the official cutting yesterday. She hadn't had chance to talk to her before their early departure and hoped that her friend had enjoyed herself. She cut a large enough slice for her to share with Robin and wrapped it carefully in a piece of kitchen towel.

"I'm just going to take some cake round to Brenda," she called up the stairs to her husband who was getting ready to go and watch a local cricket match.

"Okay, love. See you later."

Brenda was really pleased to see her when she arrived on her doorstep and invited her in, but Diane told her she couldn't stop as she needed to get back home.

"I so enjoyed the wedding yesterday. That venue was amazing, wasn't it? It was such a pity that Robin had a headache so we had to leave early."

"Oh dear. Is he in bed?" Diane looked past her friend.

"No, he left to go down to the forest early this morning. I found a note on the kitchen table when I got up saying he felt better and he would be camping out as usual."

"Well, I'm glad to hear he's all right. I must dash now as Christine and the kiddies are coming over."

Brenda watched her go, then closed the door and went back to her knitting.

CHAPTER 41

Sunday May 31st

Chloe had slept fitfully and must have checked the door lock a dozen times since she had returned from the police station yesterday. She was scared to be here on her own, but she had nowhere to go and her stalker might be out there somewhere ready to follow her. She wandered around the flat, all the time listening for any strange noises. She put on the TV, but that didn't help; she couldn't concentrate. Her hands were clenched into tight fists and every muscle in her body ached. In spite of the early hour, she helped herself to a glass of wine to steady her nerves, took a large gulp, then sat with it in the gloom of the living room with the curtains closed.

The doorbell rang. She froze. Listening, she heard footsteps on the gravel path. She got up and tried to peer out through the curtain but couldn't see anyone from this angle. Perhaps they had gone. She waited, rigid with fear. The bell rang again. She held her breath. Footsteps again. Then the door to the flat below slammed. It must have been Bob. She wondered what he wanted. She felt safer, knowing there was someone downstairs and drew the curtains back. That green car was there again. She wondered who it belonged to. Could be a dog walker, as there was a footpath nearby. She would get dressed and pop down later to find out what Bob wanted. She'd say she had still been in bed even though it was ten o'clock already.

Because she had intended to stay at her parents' until tonight, there was very little in the fridge. She remembered the chunk of the wedding cake her mum had given her for Mick so took that and ate it as she wandered aimlessly from room to room. She poured herself another glass of wine and went back to the living room, turned the television on again and half-watched some programme where a couple of interior designers were doing up houses and selling them on. Maybe it was the wine or just because she was so tired, but she fell asleep.

It was early afternoon when she woke and remembered Bob's earlier visit. She washed her face with a flannel and tepid water before going to find out why he'd called. She rapped loudly on the big cast iron knocker and waited. Bob opened the door and his face lit up when he saw her.

"I think you called earlier, but I was in bed."

"Oh yes. I was looking for your boyfriend. I was going

to ask him to give me a hand with something."

"I'm afraid he won't be here today," Chloe told him and turned to go.

"While you're here perhaps you would like a guided tour of my abode." He stood back and gestured for her to come in. "Go through to the kitchen." He pointed straight ahead. "I just want to tidy the bathroom before you see it."

Chloe walked through, looking about her at the hallway and the little area to her left, which had once been the school cloakroom and was now a completely furnished utility. Bob turned the key in the front door.

"Sorry, it's a habit. Living alone and on the ground floor, I always lock it after me."

"I can understand that - I do the same." she smiled.

"Would you like a drink? Tea or coffee - I'm afraid I don't have anything stronger."

"No, thanks." Chloe looked around the kitchen which didn't look any different to when the old lady had lived there.

"Where does that door lead to?" she asked.

"That's the cellar, all dark and full of spiders. We won't go down there."

Bob took her arm and gently steered her away from the kitchen and across the hall to the lounge, which looked out on the front of the house. There were still no curtains at the windows and very little furniture. The only piece that stood out as being new was a modern light wood veneer desk which housed a laptop computer and an angle-poise lamp.

"I think I am going to need some advice on the furnishing in here; perhaps you can help me," he said. "I've painted the walls magnolia - so easy on the eye.

Chloe didn't think she was in any position to advise on furniture so chose to ignore that comment, and said, "Magnolia is a good choice - very practical."

He shepherded her back into the long corridor which went the full length of the building and past a door on the left which looked like a cupboard. Bob quickly closed the door but not before she had seen the ghastly brown herringbone jacket hanging up along with trousers in the same material. She looked at Bob more closely and tried to imagine him in a pair of glasses.

"What was that noise?" she asked as she heard a banging sound.

"I didn't hear anything." Two doors stood on each side of the corridor, and he pointed to the open one on the left saying, "This is the bathroom."

Chloe looked in and thought it a sterile looking space. White tiles, white bath suite complete with white WC seat , white paint on the walls. The only item that was a different colour was the black vinyl tiling on the floor which looked as if it had been there forever.

"It's very bright," was all she could think of to say.

"Yes, it is," he replied as he guided her to the door opposite, which he opened with a flourish.

"This, my darling, is our bedroom."

Had she heard him correctly? She was sure she had. She looked and was completely taken aback. The room was a facsimile of her own. The same colour scheme, the same curtains, the same bedding. There was only one way he could possibly have known what her bedroom was like. He must have been in it.

She shivered.

"Chloe, this is our love nest. I have created it just for you and me." He opened his arms to show he meant the whole flat.

"Er... It's beautiful," she managed to make her voice as cheery as possible while wondering how she could escape. "I think I'll have that coffee now." She forced a smile.

He turned on the kettle and took two mugs from a cupboard, which also housed a jar of instant coffee.

"Black for me, please," she smiled from her seat at the breakfast bar.

Chloe saw her chance as he placed her coffee before her. She picked it up and threw the scalding hot liquid into his face, jumped off the stool and raced to the door - no key. She ran to the living room and managed to get to the sash window. She could hear him coming and fiddled with the catch before finally pushing the window upwards. He was right behind her. She felt his hand trying to grip her cardigan as she dived headlong into the rose bush outside. Without a thought of the pain she scrambled to her feet and dashed to her door, slamming it behind her and turning the key.

Breathless, she sat on the bottom stair sobbing. Bob was a few seconds behind her and was hammering on the door, pleading with her to come back.

"I love you, Chloe! I would never harm you."

She pushed herself up and painfully hobbled up the stairs. She found her mobile where she had left it on the kitchen table, and called the number she needed.

"Chloe, Chloe, come back." Bob was still hitting the door and she feared he would knock it down.

"DI Willis."

"Help me! It's Chloe Thornby."

"I've been trying to get hold of you. Do you know a man called Robin Hartley?"

"Yes, I do. He's outside banging on my door."

"We're on our way."

The banging and shouting had finally stopped and Chloe was worried that he had gone back to find some way of getting in using something from the big tool box she had seen in the corner of his lounge. She walked over to the window to try and see if there was any sign of him. She would also be able to see when the police arrived.

As she watched, she was relieved to see Bob, laptop case in hand, running across the road towards the dark green car, which very soon sped off up the lane.

About ten minutes later a patrol car arrived closely followed by DI Willis and a woman dressed in a business suit. Chloe ran down to the door.

"He's just left! You've missed him!"

"Stay inside and lock the door," Willis told her. "We need to check out Hartley's flat. I'll come and speak to you shortly." The uniforms and the woman had already entered the flat via the door which had been left ajar.

Chloe waited impatiently, pacing the landing and

every now and then sitting on the top stair. As soon as she heard a knock at the door she raced down to answer it, and was surprised to see Pete on her doorstep.

"What's going on? DI Willis phoned and asked me to meet him here. Have they found Karen?" he demanded as she stood aside to let him in.

"I don't know. I've just found out that my neighbour has been stalking me for the last few months and it was probably him who knocked Mick down."

As they waited they heard a siren and looked out to see an ambulance pulling into the drive behind the cop car.

"Oh my God!" Chloe shrieked and headed for the stairs with Pete close on her heels.

Willis was standing by the door of the downstairs flat, talking on his mobile. He rang off as they approached.

"I was just coming to see you. We've found Mick and Karen in the cellar. They're being taken to hospital. Karen is in a bad way and seems to be suffering from dehydration. Mick has had a nasty blow to the head. I have just been onto the force in Cheltenham to arrest Mr Hartley."

Karen was the first to be stretchered to the ambulance and looked to be unconscious. Mick walked unsteadily behind and Chloe ran to him.

"I've missed the wedding, haven't I?" he said in some confusion.

She nodded. "Don't worry about that now."

"Lock your door, Chloe. We'll follow the ambulance." Pete was already moving towards his car.

"Find somewhere else to stay for the time being," Willis advised. "I'll let you know once Hartley has been detained."

It was late afternoon when Brenda put down her knitting and went to answer the door. She wasn't expecting anyone and was most surprised to find two uniformed police officers standing on her doorstep.

"Mrs Hartley?"

"Yes."

"PC Ball and WPC Heron. Is your son Robin at home?"

"No - he's down in the Forest of Dean at the moment. Why?"

"We'd like a word with him, that's all. Does he have a mobile?"

"Yes - but he never turns it on when he's away, only if he wants to call me. He's camping you see, so he'd have no way of charging it."

"What time do you expect him back?"

"I don't really know. Not until late. He gets up early and goes straight to school in the morning so I don't see him until I get home from work."

"What school is that?"

"St Jude's Primary."

"Thank you. If you hear from him in the meantime could you ask him to drop into the station before he goes to work?"

"Yes, of course"

"Thank you"

Brenda watched them walk towards their car before closing the door and made her way back to her armchair.

I wonder what all that was about, Brenda thought as she picked up her needles.

Chloe and Pete had spent an anxious time at the hospital. Karen was confused and disorientated and had a weak pulse. The doctors acted quickly, put her on a drip and were encouraging her to drink. They would keep her in overnight. Mick was seen, his wound was cleaned, and he didn't seem to be suffering from concussion. Due to his recent accident and amnesia they were not happy to allow him to go home but finally agreed when Chloe assured them that she wouldn't let him out of her sight.

"I don't want you going back to your flat tonight, Chloe," Mick said.

"I don't want to go there either but I've only got the clothes I'm wearing and there's nowhere else I can go."

"I'll ring Mum. Have you got your phone?"

Chloe handed it over.

"That's sorted then. Dad is on his way to pick us both up."

The pattern she was knitting was a complicated one and Brenda needed to concentrate hard, causing her eyes to feel dry. She must have fallen asleep mid-row as she woke with a start when the phone began to trill beside her. The setting sun was casting an orange glow on the room and the radio was still playing away to itself.

It was Robin checking in on her - such a caring lad. He told her he had been walking for miles. In her half-asleep state she almost forgot to tell him about her visit from the police.

"I wonder what they want to speak to you about. Have you been a witness to some crime?"

"I haven't a clue," he replied. "I'll go and see them in the morning and find out."

"See you tomorrow then."

"Bye, Mum. I love you."

She would listen to the local news, then go and find some bread and cheese for supper. She thought it important to keep up with what was going on, and it was a lot less dramatic than the main news which always concentrated on bad things.

CHAPTER 42

Monday June 1st

Mick's mother had kindly made up a camp bed in her son's room and Chloe had slept soundly. Mick seemed to have suffered no lasting physical effects from his blow to the head and subsequent imprisonment in the cellar. His mum wanted him to spend the day at home with her, and it took some time and a stern word from Chloe to persuade him that it was not advisable to go to work. Chloe didn't want to go home for anything so had slept in her underwear and thought she would have to go to work in the things she had worn yesterday. Luckily, his mother came to the rescue with a decent pair of trousers and a top. They were a little too big on Chloe but they would do.

Pete rang Mick and told him that Karen had started to respond to treatment. He had stayed at the hospital until they had thrown him out and had rung this morning to be told that she was comfortable.

Mick drove Chloe to work and promised to be back at five to pick her up. She was filled with so many mixed emotions as she walked up the short drive to the farm.

"How was the wedding?" Dawn shouted as she came out through the farmhouse door on her way to the washing line.

"It was a lovely day," Chloe called back, remembering her sister's happy smile.

"I'll come and hear all about it once I've pegged these out." She indicated the large pink plastic laundry basket she was holding.

Chloe reached her office and turned on the computer. There was a pile of paperwork in her in-tray and a bundle of post on her large desk pad - a gift from one of the feed suppliers. She decided to start by opening the post and setting the paperwork within into different piles. Invoices, enquiries, and promotions from suppliers were all designated to their stack and she was about to add to them from the in-tray when Dawn came bumbling in.

"So tell me all about it. You had fantastic weather, didn't you?"

"Alex looked amazing, and the little church was beautiful, decorated with wildflowers." She smiled dreamily as she remembered but then a cloud came over her face.

"What's wrong?

Chloe broke down, sobbing as the rest of the

memories took over.

Dawn put her arm around her as she blurted out all about Mick not coming, the awful Robin Hartley and everything that had happened since. James popped his head round the door and shot off again, realising that whatever was clearly very wrong, his wife was in full control.

"My poor love. Have the police arrested him?"

"I don't know, but they warned me to be very careful and not to go home for the time being in case he came back."

"You'll be safe here," she soothed as she put the kettle on. "James and Geoff can take you to get some things later, once the animals have been fed."

"Thank you," Chloe sniffed.

Brenda had risen at her usual time of seven o clock and had put on a load of washing before enjoying her breakfast. She took some chops out of the freezer and prepared the vegetables for tonight's meal. Robin always enjoyed her improvised roast on a Monday. After hanging out the washing she just had time to listen to the half-past-eight news before leaving for work.

The planned link road at a notorious accident black-spot had been postponed yet again due to environmental issues, a man's body had been found at a beauty spot near Painswick, and there had been a rare sighting of a hoopoe bird near Lower Slaughter. The weather would remain hot and sunny for a couple of days before a front would arrive on Wednesday, bringing with it more unsettled weather. She switched it off when she heard, "Now for the sports news," and left for what promised to be a busy day at the post office.

Mick was early to collect Chloe from work and sat outside to wait in his van. James saw him there as he came across the yard, and popped over for a chat. He told Mick that they had taken Chloe to collect some things earlier.

"Geoff is built like an all-in wrestler and we both felt safe."

"Thank you. She needed some fresh clothes, but to be honest I couldn't face going back there." His face lit up as he saw Chloe coming out of the farm shop door.

James ruffled her hair as she walked round to the passenger seat, and wandered off towards the milking parlour.

"I love you so much," Mick greeted his fiancée and kissed her before starting up the motor and heading for home.

There was a knock at the door and Brenda quickly put the potatoes into the oven to roast before scurrying to answer it. She wasn't surprised to see the same two uniformed police officers standing there.

"I'm afraid he's not home yet." she greeted them as she stood aside to let them in. "You'd better sit in here, while you are waiting."

The officers followed her into the neat living room but remained standing.

"Would you care to sit down, Mrs Hartley," the female officer prompted in a soft voice.

"No - I need to see to the dinner," she replied.

"I'm afraid we have some bad news for you," PC Ball said.

She sat down, worried now and wringing her hands.

"What is it? Is it Robin? Has he had an accident?"

The officers sat side by side on the sofa at an angle to Brenda's seat.

"The body of a young man was found this morning in a car in Cranham Woods, and we have reason to believe it is your son," Ball stated.

"It can't be him. He was in the Forest of Dean last night - nowhere near Cranham."

"The car was registered in his name. I'm so sorry."

"It can't be him. He'll be here any minute, just you wait and see."

Ball left his partner with Brenda and went to the kitchen to make some tea.

"This note was found with the body, Mrs Hartley. It's addressed to you."

Brenda took the note, which the police had placed in a protective plastic wallet. Recognising her son's handwriting she began to realise that the unthinkable was true.

CHAPTER 43

Friday 24th July

Paula was going to enjoy being home for the summer and was gazing out of the window of the railway carriage, looking forward to the dig she was helping with during August at a newly discovered Roman settlement near her home town.

At Gloucester the woman opposite got off and left her Wilts and Glos Standard on her seat. Paula leant over and picked it up, and was astonished to see a photo of Mr Blue Eyes, as she had nicknamed him.

Under the photo she read:

Coroner delivers suicide verdict on local teacher
Robin Hartley, 34, a primary school teacher of St Mark's district in Cheltenham led a double life as he tried to ensnare the girl of his dreams, Chloe Thornby.

Mr Hartley followed Miss Thornby's every move and moved in to the flat below hers, covering his extended absences by pretending to be an IT professional spending his weekends there but working in Amsterdam during the week.

He bombarded her with letters and gifts over several months, but as his efforts were proving futile his behaviour became more dangerous, and it is believed that he may have tried to kill her boyfriend, plumber Michael Benfield, 35, in a hit and run last October.

Police discovered cameras, one set up above his front door and another one in the lounge of the flat where Miss Thornby lived. These had allowed him to watch her remotely from his home during the week. Hartley had also set up a fake Facebook page where he assumed the identity of someone his victim would have known from her schooldays.

On Monday 1st June, his body was found in his car by a couple walking in Cranham Woods near Painswick. A letter to his mother was found at the scene and his death has been recorded as suicide.

ACKNOWLEDGEMENTS

I would like to thank:

My editor, Lorraine Swoboda, for her sterling work with the red pen.

Dawn Johnson, for her creative design for the cover.

All my family for their continued support and encouragement.

My chums whose friendship, chatter and humour help to keep me sane.

ABOUT THE AUTHOR

Pam lives with her husband in a picturesque village in the Cotswolds district of England, where she enjoys combining her favourite pastimes of walking in the beautiful countryside and photography.

Trick of the Eye is her second novel.

Printed in Dunstable, United Kingdom